Praise for Terese Svoboda's previous

"Svoboda's fiction is marked by the same dark
language found in her poetry. . . . A sense of urgency pervades all of her work, giving the words a pulse, making her language race with insistence."—Timothy Schaffert, *Poets and Writers*

"There are writers you would be tempted to read regardless of the setting or the period or the plot or even the genre. . . . Terese Svoboda is one of those writers."—*Bloomsbury Review*

"[Svoboda's] ever-changing prose is often strikingly beautiful. . . . Postmodernism's heady potential to reinvent language, unclog the doors of perception, and reconceptualize thoughts, feelings, selves and reality is on vibrant display in this demanding, worthy novel."—*Publishers Weekly*

"The kind of satisfaction that one gets from [Svoboda's] stories is quick and blinding, governed more by instinct than reason." —Francie Lin, *San Francisco Chronicle*

"Disturbing, edgy and provocative."—*Book Magazine*

"A book of genuine grace and beauty."—*New York Times*

"Compelling. . . . The language throughout is at once potent and oblique."—*Publishers Weekly*

"Fast-paced, intense, deeply moving. . . . Svoboda uses stark imagery and the protagonist's interior dialogue to craft a most compelling and fluent narrative."—*Booklist*

"These stories shimmer and dazzle with an intensity that sometimes creates the feeling of the world as a floating, melting cloud of illusion."—Cheryl Reeves, *Feminist Review*

BISON
BOOKS

Flyover Fiction | SERIES EDITOR: Ron Hansen

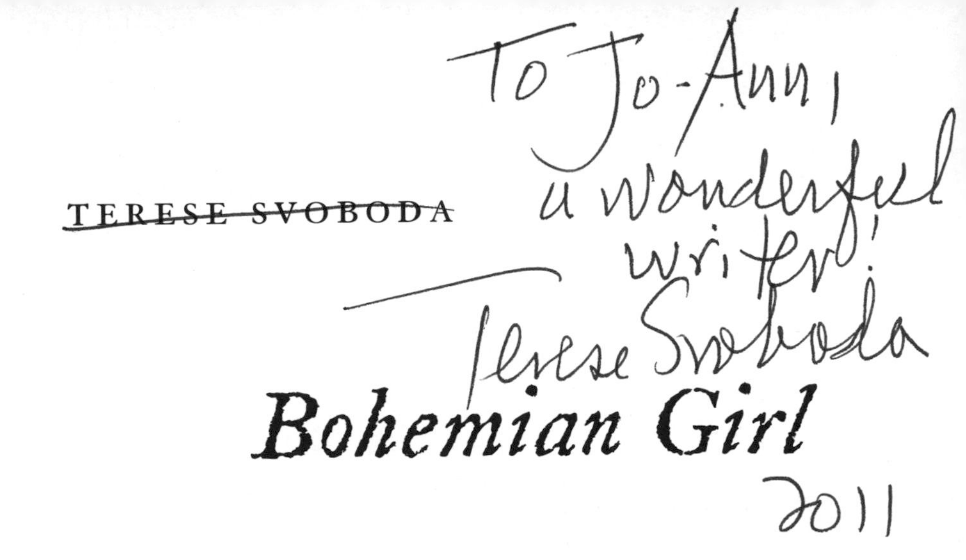

TERESE SVOBODA

Bohemian Girl

University of Nebraska Press | Lincoln and London

The author wishes to thank Steve Bull, Sondra Olsen, Gay Walley, Frank Svoboda, Ladette Randolph, Yaddo, the Bogliasco Foundation, and the Rockefeller Bellagio Center.

Library of Congress Cataloging-in-Publication Data
Svoboda, Terese.
Bohemian girl / Terese Svoboda.
p. cm. — (Flyover fiction)
ISBN 978-0-8032-2682-1 (pbk.: alk. paper)
1. Fathers and daughters—Fiction. 2. Czech Americans—Fiction. 3. Women pioneers—Fiction. 4. Resilience (Personality trait)—Fiction. 5. Frontier and pioneer life—Nebraska. 6. Nebraska—Fiction.
I. Title.
PS3569.V6B64 2011 813'.54—dc22
2011008231

Set in Granjon by Kim Essman.
Designed by A. Shahan.

To my sons, Felix and Frank

You remember how her eyes used to snap when we called her the Bohemian girl?

—WILLA CATHER, "The Bohemian Girl"

The creative Hopewell culture (contemporaries with the Caesars in Rome) flourished in North America's Midwest and raised up monuments of earth that rivaled England's Stonehenge in their astronomical accuracy.

—MARY REILLY, "What's Lost Is Found Again"

Bohemian Girl

One

Chapter 1

Pa lost me on a bet he could not break, nor would, having other daughters to do for, and other debt besides. The bet with the Indian—really a race, Pa liked any kind of bet—was who could walk first to the mouth of this river that flows so flat into the distance that the eye starts to water following it. Too thick to drink, too thin to plow, he says every time we cross it. My Pa traps and knows the land but maybe not so much the river, or maybe he stopped to take refreshment the way he does and got himself confused because that bet was not won although he and the Indian spent most of one winter chasing the river down, with the Indian squat at the mouth by the time Pa showed.

A man of honor, my Pa.

If I look into the perfect face of the river, with no rock to make a muscle in its flow or tree stump to divide it, I see Pa in it, about to haul out a trap. He trapped on land too, but rivers were his favorite. I see his face in the water and not even my true self, nor Duschecka in my arms, that's how much I want to see him. He wears a sourdough coat, a sealskin cap, and Dutch socks up to the knee, winter, spring, and fall. In summer you can know him by his short leather breeches.

I am washing Duschecka all over. She is a tree branch that nobody knows how grew arms and legs just where you would. Well, most of one leg. She broke off from the only tree growing anywhere in this prairie, with a knot on one side that could be a face. Bone-white when I found her, all her bark gone to weather and storm, heat and hoppers and deer, she turned black being in the mud a lot, like me.

I scrub her and then sink her to the river floor but I hold onto her leg the way my Pa did, teaching us swimming until we almost drowned, then I use the sand from the river bottom to clean her back to white. This slip of deer hide goes over her shoulders and down under the place where I tie a Christ knot. I call it that for it has a cross twisted into the knot if you look close. But I am not a Christ person so much as the next person, you would be surprised. The Indian who keeps me gets along fine without the Christ god, so snug and bound with His rosaries and rules. He believes instead in his own. This is all well and good but the danger in any of those gods is that in believing, people forget to do for themselves.

This Indian is trying not to let people forget to do for themselves by building a mound. Somewhere east of here is where he first saw this kind of mound, where others of his Indian kin have built them, others like the kind of relation the French and the Russians and the Bohemians have. This Indian says nobody forgets those Indians, the ones who made those big mounds, they all go on talking about them because they can still see those mounds, some about as high as our one tree, and built in the shapes of bear or crab or snake. The Indian likes the snake mound especially. It is easiest to build is what I think.

The other Indians think he builds these mounds because

he is not as happy with the gods as they are and he doesn't say no to that either. They let him go on building because he is the son of someone, and whatever he says is half his father's saying. What his father doesn't tell him but instead God, is that only women can build this mound. Since his women say he's never listened to any god before, his father's or his own, they won't build it for him, thus he is always happy to steal or trade or bet for more women.

While I am about the Indian's business, I am to keep my eyes open, Pa said, for the Indian's hoard. He said I am part of a plan to capture the hoard and make us all rich. I think Pa lost the bet so he could find out where it's hid, so I could tell him when my years are over. Four years are how many I have here to wait. The hitch is—where will Pa be when my four years finish? He's a wanderer. Some say only the French trap, but every country has its wanderers, and creatures that wander, cats with pelts people pay good money to wander after, beaver, and sometimes buffalo. Not too many trap all the way to Russia like Pa did once, or mate with people they don't have a relation to, like my Ma, who is French. One of those French soldiers who did not know Russia had the kind of winter it has, instead of marching until he nearly froze, he stayed where he saw one of Pa's traps and though he didn't die with my father's saving him, nobody could remember who he said he was afterwards. But he knew a Frenchwoman when he saw one and left a set of twins inside my Ma, twins who looked delicate like him my sisters said and who went off with him and ma.

Pa did not object after seeing how they matched, the twins and the Frenchman.

I was just small myself then, and looking like ma.

I haven't seen or heard from Pa since he whispered to me that good advice about the mound and the Indian's hoard and then left with my sisters to collect his traps and whatever else down some other river, one that Pa swore would have more luck and less debt.

His gambling habit started in Russia, a place that shelters more wolves than people. Pa is not one to save, and wolves, they never put by either which is what my brother must have meant, in resemblance. Or so my sisters said. Well, we hadn't but one slit in the Russian fort that you could watch out of to see if my brother was finding mushrooms fast enough to make up for calling Pa a wolf. All the drunk Russians crowded around the slit with us, saying he was lucky not to be beaten for saying such a thing, and some of them swore there was no wolf out there and got Pa to wager the footstool someone stood on to see out with. It turned out the mushrooms weren't everywhere near as much as they all thought, but the wolves were. Pa won that bet.

As if he wants to lose to set that straight, Pa is always saying I'll wager that the sun will rise between those trees there. Three times it happened, says Pa, that some people moved those trees, and he says he was drinking none of that clear liquor from Russia. He tries not to say vodka because it always comes out *wodka* and people here laugh. It is the medicine of Russia, he says. I am not Russian but this *wodka* of theirs is sometimes worthy of a person's debt, Pa says.

I'm a sight better off than my brother, yes I am—the Indian who keeps me, his people only talk to wolves. They don't even fear them because they say wolves are their brothers.

A brother is a little too close if you ask me.

Duschecka, Duschecka, help me dig.
Tie me to a whirl-a-gig.

This Indian who keeps me is old. I am twelve and he has two wives already who make him old. All old people have their secrets because who can know who they are or what when everything happened to them before, with no one watching from then. So far I haven't seen a lick of a hoard in any of my time here, which I tell you is making me old. It's not so bad for me but that woman way yonder was left in a trade by a husband who was in need of an Indian wife instead, and the two more you can't see are from a foolish wagon train without enough water who had to be left off. The two left behind have a brother who cannot get soldiers to look for them because the governor is being elected and he needs all his troops to parade. A younger girl named Harriet died a month after I started, gone that quick and nearly forgot, except that the Indian buried her bones deep in the mound on the sandy side.

Except for me, these females have no fixed term so it is sensible to hobble them. The Indian ties our ankles together with hide, and keeps us apart so we cannot release each other. As if a knot tightening as it dries isn't enough to keep us. As if we don't know there is no one near enough for rescue, and what the Indian might do if he caught us in an escape. With our hobbling, we can just barely move the riverbank clay or fill the water pots to soften other dirt for the mound. But I am not a complainer like my sisters who would say their lips hurt from the salt on their food. That is why my father chose me to stay and not the others.

I am limping pretty good now.

The Indian is more like Pa and does not save or store, except for bones. I think the mound is the hoard. The Indian is making it to figure out the sun, that's what he says to the others. To know more about when to plant and hunt. How can the sun falling this way or that on a mound tell you when?

But if I turn over a hoard or the mound opens with a true cross inside, how can I tell Pa? I still have it in my head the way he made me whistle for him whenever the trees confused me. Pa used his lips, loud between his teeth, as if a bird were caught there. I try that and listen for him after. The question of where Pa is ends my talk every time, Duschecka.

At least I still have my bonnet and can keep my face white so Pa can tell me apart. With its face flaps, the bonnet improves upon the kerchief. Except for its shade, you wouldn't know me from the Indians if you came to the river to water your stock. I have the braids like they do, and my clothes are theirs, and out of them stick brown arms, strong ones from hauling river mud. Sometimes I lift whole pots, sometimes I have to put them on my back—they don't care how we move them. But to work without your bonnet and have your face turn brown—even the Indians like to make their faces white at times, in the disguise of the fool god.

She is gone.

Duschecka.

Loose, she drifted from my hand. Pa is Bohemian, which means I am part of a people who fear not, but she sinks and is soon gone, and that I do fear. The water is dark from the swirled-up mud I make draining it off while I am sunk in thought. I know I will drown if I go in after her. Pa's lesson of my one leg kept out of the water taught me I will drown well enough in any water, slow or not. My hobbles prevent a chase.

Losing her makes me stop talking. I fear forgetting how with my Duschecka gone, and all the other females so distant they can't hear what flows through my head, a river in itself. I don't want to break off another branch or paddle a doll out of clay or twist her from straw like one of the other girls who had a real baby to protect and couldn't. Duschecka is just gone. Soon the land will be as dark as the water that took her and then I will go inside to forget and eat some Indian food and listen hard to what the Indian says.

I have seen no wolves here, but I have heard.

Chapter 2

The peddler could be hobbled like me. The ropes that tie on his hunchback load slip and cause him to take small steps and curse in another language. I hear him well enough but instead of raising my head and risking Indian punishment, I bend lower so he can see the last light neckskin where the bonnet band bites. My hand-insides are light too, if he cares to look, but no more my face—the sun has stole around my bonnet flaps. I bend and rinse off clay.

He is young enough it is likely his first trip.

You would think a bonnet would calm a person and make him feel the woman is on the job like a horse with blinders but so often people startle, seeing features inside, and have to stare at them to fix the face. This peddler could be expecting to see a sick red-cheeked woman or a woman grown old, the apple all wrinkled.

I tip my bonnet back.

With that bonnet lying empty on your back, you look like you have two heads, he says. He tilts his own flat hat to let the sweat fall, then he sticks his hand out from under his load. Glad to become acquainted with the both of you.

To meet his hand's sudden thrust, I trip over my broken

crock and its mud spills. Glad, I say anyway. A word I haven't heard in a long while. I untwist my bonnet and look up to his gawky black-suited self.

I have for you the finest linens, he says, and, tipping his load to the ground, he takes a seat. Even if you are not in immediate need. He stares at my hands. What lamb are you to tolerate this forsaken place?

I sit beside him and pull in my skin dress so it hides the big rip that is starting where it oughtn't. I shove my ankles together so the hide-hobbles look as if they are a part of shoes.

Who you be really? he says in the wait, until he looks around for an answer from somebody else.

Nobody else is what he sees. A beaver or a badger at best, relocating themselves downriver.

I work at a word. Camphor, I say.

I have that, he laughs. That's not your name.

I could read it on a box, when I could read, I say.

A reader, he hmmms. He begins to put out what he's brought in his load. Well, Missus Reader, this here is soap, this here is dry goods. I never met a lady who could resist the dry goods, especially one in a bonnet on a hot day with nobody to talk to.

He throws out a smile of such a size that I think maybe he has trouble with the selling. He must know he will have trouble with me, since he doesn't see a scrap of hide or fur I could barter, except what I wear. Maybe he's practicing. He is not much older than I am so he must need the practice.

You been selling long? I say.

He smooths a pantleg. It is the goods that sell themselves anyway, not me, he says. Some days Indians will take a bale of dry goods off my back with no apparent need, and the next day I will see the cloth I sold spread against the door of a tent, used as a spill fan. Once I traded a cattle brand for three buffalo hides. The Indian was in the possession of a bull he needed marked as he had rightfully gotten it in payment from white men looking around for what they would find if he would find it for them. He was a scout. I am hoping to make such a trade more than once.

He finds Camphor in his load and puts it down in front of me. Maybe the someone who jars it up is called Camphor, he says. I reckon it's Latin anyway for something to do with throats, or covering up smells.

I am sniffing his jar, big deer sniffs.

Say, he says, screwing the lid down tight as if I stole something. I hear there's a lot of Indians up this way. You know what kind?

My Pa warned me, I say.

Yes? he says. Camphor with rectified spirits, he reads. Take it to allay irritation.

Pa said I should listen to what Indians listen to and I would get along better. Be careful, he said to me, there's always someone coming who will try to tell you otherwise. I watch the peddler close. You know my Pa?

That is just the thing a Pa would say, he says, while he repacks one thing and another.

Pa, I say, and clutch at him. You got some idea where he's at?

The fellow backs down and confesses he does not know where my Pa is, or anyone like him.

They don't have the need or the want of goods like yours anyway, I say. Pa and the girls.

You don't know that, he says. He buckles on his load.

I have only a year left, I say. What exact year are we in?

He lurches to his feet with his bundles, slipping in the muddy sand. We are in the Christian Year of Our Lord 1861 and the month of June, the day of which I do not know myself, and I mean not to fall prey to unfriendly Indians nor to the vagaries of the war we are fighting which is probably where your Pa is today.

Vagaries, I say. It is only 1861, I say. The same year two years after I began. I grip my fingers tight to his coat flaps. Are you sure?

I must make talk with these friendly squaws yonder, he says, backing up the bank at a skip, his load almost crushing him, his ropes slipping while he wildly ties them.

I pull his pantleg so hard he falls flat to the ground, his burden crashing off his back. He lands on his tailbone, which landing affects his speech with curses flat out terrible. I get the gist: Oy, you bugger-eyed, squander-headed, mashed brain of a female, I curse you and your bonnet too, may your teeth get angry and chew off your head, Gehenna. Then he falls quiet, feeling for his aches and bones, his misery not wanting in pain.

I got no reason to torture you, I say, emptying my crockful of sand onto another pile of it. No apparent reason, I mean. I am in need of a disputation.

I give that word some spit, hardly remembering it.

What? he says, still feeling his bones.

I take a breath in quick as if only a lot of air will let me lift my hobbled leg, which he has not noticed before as I have kept them both so tucked. I want you to help them understand this. Pa gave me to the Indian to honor a bet. It is my honor that is bound, not myself.

You should run off, he says, and he leans back and finds a pocket in his pants where his knife is hid and takes it out.

No, I cry, seeing that knife. You don't understand honor either. The Indian must be the one to free me. Or why I am here is broken.

You don't know that, he says, feeling the knife edge.

I do. Make the Indians understand I am an honorable slave, I say. No one here has been able to do that, though some have tried.

There are others? He scans the view for its promise of sales.

I point far off, toward two approaching Indian women. They are like me, without means.

He shifts his flat hat so more of his sweat line shows.

You can almost hear the Indian ladies' bell leggings ring, they are quick getting that close. The Indian put bells on them to warn himself that they are coming. The Indian is smart in the ways of females, he must be, since they so much do not like what he is building.

The peddler glances over at the long mound, its hill state. I only know this and that in the Indian language, he says. He turns the knife in his hands as if he will still find something for it.

I look at him and his small insect position on the ground. Please ask for me, I say. Tell them what I want.

They are pretty good with the breaking of horses, I don't see why a girl like you shouldn't be allowed to run, he says.

Have you not been listening? Honor is the point of this.

The two Indian women do not stare but come right up and lift up their hands in front of them.

That means *What are you doing here?* I say.

It shows they have no weapons, he says. That is good. Why, one Indian was so out of sorts with the removal of so many of his kin that when I offered a nice load of blankets, he came at me with the hatchet I had sold him the last time.

Ugh, he says to the women. Ugh, he says, pointing at me. He puts out and up his hands, he shovels at the river with his arms and at my hobbles, he slaps on a pretty good smile.

The bigger of the two women, the one wearing a rag from someone lately taken off a wagon, smiles too. She motions and he motions and they both smile again.

I think she thinks I want to marry you, he says.

I laugh the way an animal would, short, deep in my throat. That's always what men think women are talking about.

You tell them yourself then, he says, turning away. He looks around at the sand, at the water, at the hot sun overhead. I need a nap. He stretches out.

The smaller woman brings out her knife.

I am not really a bit sleepy, he says, sitting up. He picks up his load, he staggers, swinging it back into position.

Tell my Pa not to forget me, I say, as he heaves forward. You will know him from his daughters. They all look like me. Maybe I have an eye color, maybe even a way of talking that my sisters use too. If we all wore the same bonnet, I call out, I suppose it would be easier.

When he turns, I think it is to see whether the women are going to scalp him or if they are going for me instead, and only last to see what I look like. The picture he gets is a girl with braided hair and a hobble around her ankles standing beside a mound of clay, dirt, and sand, with the lady Indian throwing the knife into the mound she hates it so much.

He blocks the sun a while.

Chapter 3

The mound needs strength.

The Indian tamps his pipe bowl. Its long straight stem is new, its length wrapped in telegraph wire some other Indians found beside a pole. Or so they said. What was it doing beside the pole and not strung on it? is what he asked. He collected the pipe bowl by riding eight days to the quarry where he met his fifth brother, William the Hat, who listens now even while he sleeps which is what he likes doing best—a nice soft deerskin, a smoky shelter, who could not? William the Hat sighs in the happiness of his half dream and says out loud: The bones of the slave are what strengthens the mound. Leg bone, arms, skull—in the two years she lays there, the mound has not washed away.

Slaves do their best work alive, says the Indian.

William the Hat takes his turn at the pipe. They do not think that in London, he says. The bridge there is said to have many bones in it, the workmen's, even the children of the workmen. It is very strong. They walled them in alive.

They must have a lot of workmen. I still wonder why she died from that mushroom, says the Indian, shrugging.

A mushroom that is not even bad. It can give you stomach trouble, yes, but worse are unripe beans.

You can't keep them from Indian food.

True, says the Indian. I trade for the whitest flours and even once a nice strawberry-and-sugar—

Jam.

Jam. They think we are stronger with our food.

We are just stronger. But you should see the mounds that whites make in their cities. Eagle-nest-high. Mon-u-ment, William the Hat says in three parts.

I would go to see these cities, their *ments*, says the Indian, but their women tempt me. Horse Fat knows this. She caught me wearing a blanket over one arm like a bachelor.

William snores. He is not wearing the derby he prizes, the only souvenir for his time of captivity he did not give away. It lies beside him, a small dark animal curled up at the edges.

The Indian stirs the coals red and relights his pipe. Umbrel-la. Giving the god-forgotten wire-bird-trees to everyone so everyone would think they were crazy and not you—so clever, William. Um-brel-la. No one stoned you like they did the Indian who traveled there and came back with just one clock.

Stoning, always the stoning, says William, turning on his side.

I say, let's show off the slaves the way they do us when they catch us. That is my new idea since you have come. Let's put them in our clothes and take them around. Others will feed us for a chance to see slaves dressed like this.

Servants, says William. They like to be called servants.

They could eat their own food and we could make them wear paint and feathers the way we dressed for last year's sex dances.

No one will believe they are white. Look at their skin now—as brown as yours.

The two men watch the smallest as she enters with a haul of buffalo chips.

She is unripe, says the Indian. And ugly—such small feet.

Bonnet shreds lie limp around her neck. She squats and lets the buffalo chips fall out of her doubled shirtfront.

You increase your feeding expense if you produce another they can't take away, says William. Half-breed. He is sitting up now, reaching for his turn at the pipe. Some go back to the whites and betray us.

You did not betray us.

William the Hat looks into his smoke. I am not half.

You are half changed by your time with them, says the Indian. We should have stoned you.

William pretends to snore, his smoke escaping his nose.

After arranging the chips in the fire, the girl stands quickly and then stands too long, waiting for the word *Go*. The Indian takes her by the arm and feels its strength.

My ankles hurt, says the girl. She likes to say this whenever the Indian takes an interest.

Can't you see her in front of the fire saying *Mi nklz urd* for everyone? says the Indian.

William the Hat's eyes open again. That's the kind of thing I did for their queen. I said, Look, there's an antelope over and over. Though sometimes I said, Your queen is a smelly fetus. And dance—they had me lifting my feet until they ached.

People here will pinch her to see what sound she makes. The Indian pinches her arm.

My ankles, she says again. She shuffles in her hobbles, she stamps in them.

She and the others could be trained to dance for other tribes, says William. We could see many more women if we traveled around and not just the rejected ones, the ones who end up forsaken here, that's what the peddler says.

He can talk? says the Indian. I would never let him close to the women if I knew he could talk.

I traded with him for some of that twisted string. Lace? That's the word. I remember when I need it. I'm going to prick my hat and hang the lace there.

William touches his hat brim.

If only I could use men to build this mound for me. The Indian makes a puff of smoke, still not letting her go. But in my dream of it, only the women build.

You sleep less than I do—that is what makes you crazy. Our women won't build no matter what your dream. It is one job too many. Besides, I have heard that the men building those mounds where you saw them could not stop once they started, and no one found food and they starved.

Men are stupid.

She leans away from the Indian, toward the door, she leans hard. He releases her. Her hobbles catch on William's hat and she stumbles, falls, rights herself, all angles of rawhide and elbow, over William.

You see, she loves me, says William. She doesn't want to leave.

What is she always saying with this *Mi nḳlz urd*?

William appraises her. She is saying the queen is a smelly fetus.

They laugh into their smoke, they wipe their eyes.

Where is my father? she says in Indian.

The two men go quiet. She understands—what?

You know that is not all clay you are moving, says William. Some of it is *tour j'ete*. He puts on his most impassive face, which to anybody Indian means this is a joke.

She doesn't know the English for *tour j'ete*. He doesn't know that not all whites understand all their languages the way he knows most Indians'. She says in English, My father is this tall, and holds her hand high, over her head.

I have not had a good bet since I won this slave, says the Indian. You are not granted liquor drinkers every season, the ones who say they know everything. To her he says, Will you bet on the day of your release?

She limps out, her face as impassive as William's, which means she is sorry to know any of their words, *father, how long, liquor*.

After two more draws on his pipe, the Indian says, To eat their deaths is a quiet way, is it not?

William pets his hat like some men do their chest hair. This ankle girl, he says, will not wear out or be stupid about eating. She knows she will be free when her time ends, which makes her bones strong, which makes hers best for the mound.

The Indian smokes.

The court once sent me to where the slant-eyed people traded, says William. They wanted me to work for one of them but once they saw the size of me and heard how much I could eat, I was returned. It was from them that the court bought a medicine that makes you dream-crazy. Maybe she could take this medicine and stay. I am sure the peddler knows how to trade for it, this crazy-dream, or something the same. Why, he walks to where the land ends, where all that water starts, the way I did.

By the time he returns, says the Indian, many moons or so, I will have the mound stretching much farther and as tall as two men, I will have the head of it hissing into the land. Everyone will know everything about the sun from it. Still, there will be the bends of the tail to build.

William the Hat blows into the smoke. Why a snake, why not an eagle or even a beaver? A beaver with such a tail, and a mound he builds himself?

The Indian puffs harder before he answers: The snake has no legs so it can't be made into a man. And its head is now, its tail is later.

Ah, says William, and shakes his head. People are talking that you are just making a bad wall. That's what they don't like. They fear it.

People fear each other, shrugs the Indian. We all fear God. The Indian reaches into a pouch hanging from his neck and shows William the magic he has in it. It is the face of this girl, old, inside a gold clam.

William puts his hand to his mouth. She is in there too?

William, says the Indian. Haven't you seen these clams in your travels?

Yes, yes, he says as if he is really yawning and not letting his own fear out. But such a likeness. Maybe it is her mother.

It floated downriver in the pocket of the clothes of a man, just the clothes drowned in the spring waters we get from up there. No doubt a bet the man wouldn't give up or he slipped in or was pushed. I would bet on that last.

The waters of spring. William takes the face in his hand. He could have bet his clothes.

The Indian sucks his teeth, that's how much he doesn't doubt it.

She could leave now, William says, after adding another coal to his pipe. A man doesn't owe more than his life reaches. If this is so.

To hear news that he could be dead will not free her. Where will she go anyway? Indians move in the land as far as you can walk, all the way to the pipe quarry. Someone else will keep her if we don't.

Give her up. Her people are coming. A circle of wagons full of idiots starve only two days' walk farther.

She can't see their fire.

William returns the pipe. She might choose her death like the other with the mushrooms and take you too. There's treachery in *Mi urz*, just in the sound of it.

The Indian laughs and it is a laugh that no one should make, a laugh that drives all the other Indians but William away.

William puts the hat on. Two sizes too large, it is a raven nesting.

She has no choice, says the Indian. Time has stopped for her—the Indian finds his heart with his hand as if he is putting it back inside—and now she carries the dirt for herself.

Chapter 4

At first the drops bounce when they hit—you can see them coat with dust, resist like silver metal in gobs, pull away—then they pool and run all the way down the leaves onto my shoulders and then my bound hands.

I am tied to the tree Duschecka came from. The few leaves summer has left it release more of the shower after the rain stops, but many of its limbs lie stacked at my feet—the Indian wants to burn me.

I know it is close to the day of my release. The peddler helped figure the actual day when he stopped here just after the tree had taken bud, his usual time. The Indian had beaten him for bringing the wrong thing. No one else complained about his dreams after having drunk whatever it was, the peddler said, but your Indian said he wanted different dreams. You were supposed to try it too, said the peddler.

I hardly sleep, I said to him. I need to measure the days right.

After he left, I keep track of the days myself. The Indian knows it is my day approaching and has talked to me in his white voice, the voice a little higher than his Indian one, as if

I have to be reached with a voice from home, and says I am his wife already, I cannot go.

When am I his wife? Drinking a nut drink, or standing on a deerskin facing the moon? Asking him if he can give me more water? Or bound to the tree with these boughs piled around, dancing in place what I believe is a dance for rain? No preacher will say that we are married, and he has not touched me, which is what he agreed to with Pa, that long ago.

My fingers work at the rawhide ties that bind me. They are wet from the rain, and maybe I can stretch them and force my fingers between. One of the other girls used rawhide ties under her bonnet strap, dying so quietly while they dried and tightened that not even the squirrels bothered her. I found her, empurpled above where the dried hide cut. She had no release to look forward to like I did. The Indian buried her bones in the second crick of the mound just past where Harriet's are put. He rendered flesh from bone first and when the other two died—one from slipping so hard in the flat river that she struck a rock, and one taking sick after a hand burn—he did the same.

The will of the mound, Amen and Alleluia. I am still alive and it is time for my deliverance. I will not work and I will not sicken. That the Indian chopped down so much of the only tree he has shows how much he wants me to stay, and either way he wants my bones. He has gone crazy about bones, believing his god wants them to make the mound strong. I tell him he should get more female slaves.

Fewer are left behind, he says. Some brother or husband will kill me if the women have to be taken by force.

He's cinching my hands together around the tree.

If they kill me, he says, getting the gist of my glee at some brother or husband or even father advancing in defense, I won't come back and you won't ever be free. Dance, he says. Lift those feet.

I danced, tied to the tree.

The Indian also believes in signs. Well, that rain I danced for, bound and tied, and that for once came, was his sign all right. It is his problem if he thinks his god brought it, if he thinks at last I can make rain with God.

Oh, the songs we girls did sing together, with our feet falling on the words they gave us. God should have wept his rain back then. The Indian has become very fussy about his god in the last few moons, which is lucky for me. While he was waiting for Horse Fat to bring a spark from their fire to the wood at my feet, the rain started falling and they all fled. A sign! A sign! they shouted, with him the loudest.

I almost have the knot lifted, the end is pulled around my small finger, the one with a catch in it from all the hauling.

Ducks fly in foolishly and stay to look at their feet on the wet ground. They will get cooked on all this wood by the fire Horse Fat will bring that might still be mine when the rain stops if I can't work my way out fast enough.

I work hard.

Every day for a year, the Indian used a locket as a magic over me. He pulled it from a pouch and stared at its insides and talked to me when he was sure I was listening. He made certain I knew what he said: that the mound was strong, stronger than a white man's mound, that I did not need to see myself old inside the clam, its magic was not mine, that my Pa had sent him this clam to keep, to double my strength. He used the locket so often to talk to me that Horse Fat spat on it. The other wife said only that he is having more visions, he is worse than ever and should be taken to a far pasture, but she only whispered it.

William the Hat finally buried that locket. He dug a place out of the mound for it at night while the Indian was not watching, William the Hat foreswearing this or that at the time, a lot of religious rigamarole that would make its burying as potent as the bones'.

At least it was gone and the Indian calmer.

My hand is almost out.

I have heard not one word from my father or sisters. If not visit, they could at least make time in a dream or in a thought that I haven't already turned over.

A lark comes to sit at my side to make noise at the ducks. My second sister transformed? That is what I think often enough. Or one of the others, in a state? Oh, I will fly too.

I'm not going to unearth the locket before I go although it is my mother's and I know where it is because it fell out once, the clay mix not being so strong there, the sand crumbling. I moved it to a place only I could know. Knowing is the same as having. I could not let myself be caught with it. Besides, I can't take such a thing that Pa should have. If I can't find Pa having it, it seems wrong for me to have it.

They don't know it's not me.

William the Hat said as much when he had the women hold me down to dress me for the last dance before this one. You have seen her old face in the gold clam? he says. Soon her smoke will join with the pipe's to make the mound stronger, the way her old clam face already has.

I bit him. Besides his smoky talk of the clam, I would not dress one more time for that dancing. I had had it with dancing. Every two bucks and their families came to see me dance their dances and say my name the way they did and make their war cry, and cry *My ankles hurt*.

My ankles do.

It is a dark rain now, a daystorm of wind and blackness rushing in to fill around that single rain cloud. The storm tears at the Indian's sleeping place, where he and the others must watch. But the sky will lighten soon enough—the ducks walking off is a sign. I see signs too, but not from God.

He wanted so much to burn me, he would even burn a tree. The only one. Duschecka's.

I had come to like him and his careful building, his Indian and not-so-Indian ways. After all, he spent time with Pa, and Pa liked him. And he let me teach William the Hat a Bohemian song, though words I used were American: *Uncle Sam will give each of you a farm*. Very popular, I remember my oldest sister saying, giving it the only tune we knew.

I twist my hand free and pull out the other.

I hold out hope in front of me and it isn't some bar of lye and fat and ash congealed together and melting now against the fast rain, a soap I've forgotten how to use. I crouch and rip the hobbles from my ankles—my honor absolved—I stretch my legs out full, and I take off limping.

Chapter 5

I walk east. East is my best guess since that is where Pa lit out after leaving. I take off east along the river, until I come upon another river branch and take it too. I walk beside it print-less, on brush and stones and sometimes in the water itself, with my hide shoes, wet or dry, leaving no lame mark an Indian might be tempted to track, the way they taught me. At night I bend down the long grass and sleep in a curl so the grass jumps up without a sign of any sleeper, another Indian way.

It is noon the next day when I stop again and think out all that I've seen, birds going this way, a wagon track older than myself, and sixteen prairie dogs blinking at me as one from their doorway sentries. Where they look toward they mark danger and what is danger to a dog is not good for me either. Of course I come from the way they watch and of course they worry over me too, and maybe I'll let them.

Will I know my sisters? I say to the dogs astride their hard holes. Will I? Will I?

The dogs shuffle and blink but do not budge.

I want to see a boat, I tell them. Pa talked of boats sometimes when we checked traps, about how you could go anywhere on one on an ocean, right, left, or center, with no trees in the way, no mountains, but with current pushing, yes, like on a river, a current to take you where it will, and the same with wind. We all remembered riding in a boat to get up the river, that going on a boat was more like walking a trail. But I was too young on the boat we took to cross the ocean, the one that goes anywhere with wind and current. What about that kind of boat for here? There is wind.

I hold my hand against it to show the dogs but they all disappear.

I limp off again, around them.

I could use some meat. Not dog-meat, that is tooth-proof, you can't get it soft enough to swallow no matter if you boil it a whole day and then beat it. Often enough even an otter steak is too tough if you don't get to it soon enough. If it is too long a time between the dying of the animal and the removing of the jacket of fur, you will taste the bitter innards too. Remember how those fresh eyes turn, taking off that jacket? But sometimes it is fear that spoils it. At our feet would be some wolf or possum or beaver thrashing and screaming or not stiff yet with its leg bit half off or its eyes staring or worse, its fur in shreds, with the pink gore fresh on top, and its little ones coming in close, sniffing and crying too, and then the animal is not worth the effort, dining or otherwise, the fur so ruined, only fit for a legging, and the meat too tough even to boil up the fear that the blood inside makes in it.

I have no fear now. The Indian gave me so much fear at the end, it came in buckets until I had no choice but to drink it down and be Bohemian.

I walk right into the blue of this country's sky, the color of the glass Bohemians keep one or two bottles of in every house. If I had any sense I would change my skin and clothes to this blue so no Indian could find me, new or old. I could be a walking blue and lost to the eyes of all. One of the girls working with me told me there is a berry that will stain blue and a stain like that will stay on cloth and on a person's face until you scrub it hard. I will search for those berries, I say to the blue sky. I will pass through this country the way we used to, coming upon this and that, and then I will see Pa or at least a sister in the furs they surely still trade, and I will walk right up to them without the ado you are always having when you are away and there those bushes of blue will be. I will say that is all I am looking for, not them.

The ground keeping up all that blue sky has about as much grass thick on it as the whiskers a young boy could shave. Or so it appears to me. My eyes still water from the thick smoke night after night inside the Indian's sleeping house—my place was close to the fire, good for the heat, yes, but hard on the eyes. What is that in the midst of that blue? Turned sideways it gives up a chimney shape but full across it is a walking black staircase of bones and a neck.

Such a horse walking up to me is the sign of the lonesomeness of its life. It walks up and I kiss the soft black hairs dragging at its neck, then it doesn't take off when I grip its mane and lever my lame leg over its back and struggle up. It is as if I am climbing a soft hillside, warm and breathing.

The walking step of the horse and the height of it lull me after all my time laboring at the level of the ground. The horse's long black back is built for sleep without taking a fall, a good slope, although I do not calculate that, I just find my eyes turned to the back of my head, hard against it.

This horse knows where he is going. I wake to a nice trickly creek in the dark where people have camped and left coals cooling, which means a fire for me for one thing, and for another, tracks if not people I can follow away from it, though the horse probably won't want to follow them anywhere as tracks will only lead to more work for it.

I am too tired to go after those people now. So is the horse. I lean up against the horse's back where it chooses to lie down beside the fire I coax up. I have never known a horse to relax like this at night so this one must be dead tired on its feet like me. Its heart inside thumps and its lungs wheeze against my ear where I lay against it. Resting, I eat small bits of the Indian bread I have kept secret from myself, hardly chewing it down so I won't think twice and get cautious and spit it out and save it for later.

Other people would pray. I know that.

Scripture and all that clap you look for in an instance like this wasn't for me even before I danced for those Indians, for every single Indian that came around, and the rain fell as often as I danced or didn't, when my little belief changed into a ball you could throw at the sky. That it rained when I was ready to be burnt explained only how a person can be surprised. What did the girls say Harriet told them at her last, after eating those mushrooms? Onions were her favorite food because they came so well wrapped, with something escaped from the middle. The Lord is like that, wrapped and wrapped, always escaping, she said, and with Him being the sneaking-off shepherd, I am left being the sheep. And then she died. I found a sheep once with its foot caught in rock, just standing there with night coming on quick. Which night always does in such a caught situation.

Horses eat in the night. I know this too. Will this horse struggle up and eat while I roll off its side? I place a pile of ripped weeds next to its head so it can chew lying down and not wander off in its hunger.

I will say nothing about the black horse to anyone when I get so old I have that face in the clam and have to use a cane to walk with. I will say I limp from the dropsy and nothing more. Your life is your own business and when they ask why or how did you get to be in Baxter or some such town, at such an age with such a horse, I will chew my lip the way I did a deerskin for the Indian and if I must, say only the Lord did not help. Bravery when you have no choice is worth less if you brag about it.

It is not the horse's eating that wakes me. Two soldiers take away the horse. Their brass buttons, or the few they have left, glitter high enough in the moonlight that I know they are as tall as soldiers should be from where I am flopped to the ground after the horse lifts his neck. I have never seen this kind of soldier before, ragtag and by themselves. They sure aren't worried about bothering me, especially with guns slung on their shoulders, though how can they be that good aiming them in the night? *Giddyup*, they say to the horse as if they have just left him there to rest, and he leaves me.

I am almost stepped on where I fall. The two of them circle the horse with a rope that he nickers against, they say they don't want no trouble, one after the other, just to stand aside.

I'm no good at just standing, I bother the horse so he won't be caught, I *who-ha* him off. Lady! they say and I'm surprised that they see through my Indian ways but they are just as surprised I bother them.

Have you seen my Pa?

Pa! They laugh into the blackness. One of them says, We

have seen nothing, and we hope to see more nothing. You understand?

This one catches the horse despite me, but after the other soldier climbs up behind him, he throws down his pack. You are always doing this, the other says short to him. Then the horse gallops away nice as if the two of them aboard were what it was waiting for.

It is no kind of pillow, this pack, but in daylight I find it's fat with food and a hand-drawn map that shows a fort practically stuck in the river ahead, and, if I turn that way and squint, seeable if you know where to look. A hat is wedged inside the pack too, a soldier's with a cavalry brim. I shove it low on my head against the sun. Though the pack is close to a horse's burden or a crock full of dirt, I haul it anyway.

I have to choose between the soldiers' tracks and the old ones. Both start off close but split in the distance. I don't try the soldiers'. You don't night-steal and threaten a girl when the lazy life of a fort is your aim. I choose the old track and stop a few steps on, crane around and pull my skirt forward for a look.

There is all this blood on the back.

I am not cut or hurt. I find where it flows and wipe it with weed and wipe it again. I mind the blood but what am I to do? No one has shed it but myself.

Going along way past the river, a heavy wagon gets involved in the old tracks and though I fear it is one that carries cannonballs the tracks run so deep, I lay my belief in it carrying cream, very heavy cream, and I follow it.

Chapter 6

The six lean-tos that make up the town called Mt. Airy according to the pasteboard dug-in sign are just wagons taken apart and nailed into houses. Pa could have passed by the town even before the wagons were taken apart—or long before, when the land held up no pasteboard sign at all. With just about a dead snake's worth of wriggle left in me and no food, I walk around calling out Pa! and am half gone away even at my pace before they say *Sit*.

They could've said *Beg*.

Two girls and a baby are all that come out of the lean-tos to say this *Sit*.

Pa who? says the girl without the baby, a girl whose hair is red. The other girl says they have biscuits, not your Pa. A biscuit. And a piece of buffalo hardtack that will take the wind out of you to chew. Not that you have much wind.

They sit too on the pounded-down dirt in front of their door.

The baby gives me the eye whilst I eye them back. That baby can really eat, is what the eye says. The baby eats the biscuit they held out for me.

We come from Bulgaria says the tall girl, putting the baby

down now that the baby wants the hardtack too. And you are from where?

The truth I could say is that I was lost way back before the tracks split and the horse left with the silver-buttoned soldiers and I had my spell of dizziness from the blood going out of me. But I am wary. I am a war girl, I say, pointing at my cap.

You know you are on the free side now, says the red-haired girl.

I stand instead of answer. A war girl should not sit and leave blood spots. Yes, I say. But I am sure I don't want to be free. I want to be with Pa and my sisters.

My mother fired a gun once, says the girl, who is now fingering back her caterwauled red hair to show a real ribbon hidden inside.

Once. The other girl, the tall one, fusses with the baby. She says her mother killed her brother with the gun, the brother who was coming for the father. We are cousins, she says.

The baby makes the dust dance by kicking its feet.

Pa, I croak again.

The two girls look at the baby, not me.

Do you have water? I ask.

We will not tell you where it comes from because then you will leave us, says the one holding the baby's foot. Here is our canteen instead.

I do not deny that I would leave but I am very happy to drink, and drink from the canteen and feel my insides swell. I've half a mind, I say, to sleep.

I mostly sleep for two days until the light changes when the weather does. I wake and pull myself in tighter in their lean-to, its cave where they all—the father, the mother, the girls, and the baby and myself—tangle together on the floor or on the little dugout shelves where you have the cut earth to smell when you turn. The baby wants less sleep in the night and even less in the day, but someone tricks it in the night with a sugar tit, a cloth dipped in colic medicine strong enough in liquor to catch fire, and a rocky corner of sugar. Two sucks and the baby goes limp and quiet until the light changes and the weather, and then he too wakes up for good.

The baby is wiggling on his back when I see him, his hands high in the air as if they are tied with string. There is this sudden play of lightning in daylight, that kind of weather, and that's what the hands play in, and I call out to hear who is where.

The girl with thc red hair and the ribbon, not the tall one, is all there is to watch the lightning with me.

Thank you, I say, seeing my skirt all rinsed and dried beside the fire, and myself in a shift. I hook the clean skirt on and do my business outside between lightnings where the girl says to go, and I see nobody else. I look for others, I go from lean-to to lean-to, but no one stands or sleeps in any of them.

There are no chairs anyway.

The girl is still where I left her. Someone came through talking about the new gold and all of them quit for it. No one else had to hear about it twice except us.

The baby flails when she says *us*. The girl dangles her bonnet tails over the baby for him to fidget with.

Together we set off to find the others in the field before it rains. The lightning keeps crossing terribly in the dark morning. Maybe they need help in the field with the horse, says the girl. I take the baby because it makes such a choking cry left behind. But this baby isn't like sand that you scoop once and then drop quick. It waves its arms at the lightning and that makes it heavy, heavier. *Stop* is what it might be saying, in Bulgarian hand signs, and with all its heaviness.

Walking far over the stiff clumps of turned dirt and grass, we finally find the family, every one of them flat to the ground, dead. Only the plough stands and behind it is where the mother has fallen in her harness. The father's hand holds a hatchet that he used in putting the corn into the rows, and the mother holds him and the girl, as if she is telling them both it is no use, the land doesn't want them and neither does the sky, just the lightning. The girl clings to the mother as if to keep her back. They are all dead of lightning. They must be dead because the rain hits hard at the father's open eyes.

We make our wet way back to the lean-tos, we grasp for each other, almost squeezing the baby sick between us. The baby does cry.

After the rain lets up, the best we can do for burying is in the turned-over soil beside where they fell, where the rain and the plough have softened it. The digging is easy enough for me, I have been digging like this for four years. I tell the other girl to talk to the baby about how we have to put dirt over his Ma and that the darkness has come and such, though it cries as if it already knows this. I try to put him to the mother's cold breast before I bury her but either the milk has already gone solid or the baby doesn't like it cold because as hungry as he is, he won't take it. The girl settles the baby on the bank with the mother's shoe at his mouth and sets to copying the names from the front of a Bible onto boards left over from their wagon, using a hard piece of charcoal good for about two rains.

When the boards are shoved upright into the soft earth, the girl tosses back her red hair and says, I am Sharon, kin to them all.

Harriet is my name, I say back. It doesn't seem right to have anyone call me by the name Pa used until he claims me. Harriet is handy.

He is Hudgins, Sharon says but she says she never calls him anything but Baby.

We go back and tear through the other lean-tos for anything useful. All we turn up is one of those lockets that women like my mother liked, to show they belonged to someone but here there's no picture, only hair inside, wiry black locks that spring out as soon as I pry hard at the hinge. I am surprised it is left behind but Sharon says they were in a powerful rush, and she takes it. I don't begrudge her, but I don't tell her about the one of my mother the Indian had, the only sign of her in the world I know. I look instead for all the other things I am missing, and they are still.

The dead family's lean-to shows them eaten into their stores, not a penny's worth of pork side left, and only flour dust at the bottom of a box. We do find a wad of dough souring in a left-out cutdown barrel in the lean-to, which we put to cooking. The fire, made of lean-to wood, flares up at a late point and scorches the bread. We go back out into the field and pull up some corn that has taken hold where the father has chopped into the earth, but the boiled shoots give us the aches. We drink all the rest of the colic medicine and rub in all the liniment. In the day's first darkness, we give the baby the last hunk of sugar and he shreds the tit with his sucking.

What is wrong with here? I ask Sharon in the morning.

She looks up from patting the baby's back hard for its

crying. This town was not meant to be, she says. Their idea was to stake four good corners and meet all their claims at a point, but they stopped where they wore out and left for the gold. Now it is just so many feet by so many feet, a place to file on.

Where else is there in the way of towns around here? I ask. I am not used to looking for them.

Since I came on a wagon behind a leader, she says, I couldn't say what or how we passed and know nothing about what is ahead. Just the river.

There are ruts, I tell her. I have a map with a fort drawn on it.

Then you lead the way, she says. We can leave the baby.

I look down at his wrenched mouth, his stiff fists. Already Sharon has the mother's spare apron tied on and the father's nails in her pockets and is turning herself away from the signboard with Mt. Airy across it.

They are all the rest dead, I call out. But this baby.

Sharon rubs her arm and moves her head in a slow yes. We should leave the Bible too, she says. Too heavy.

I lift the baby to my back and tie him on like an Indian. The baby stops his crying.

Here, I say to Sharon, take my pack.

We are lucky and locate the river first and drink from it, the baby lapping, getting water in its eyes. Then we walk on the ruts beside it backwards to confuse the Indian, and I teach Sharon to shuffle on the brush and smooth our prints. The Indian can always guess where I'm headed but maybe his mound is so soft from the hard rain that came with all the lightning that its mud has slid onto where he sleeps. It did not in all the time I worked on it but it could have. He could have to heave the sand and mud himself off his sleeping place while his wives move all their belongings. He may be busy now but two girls walking away might be seen as slaves more than ever. I walk fast with that baby and Sharon legs it, having only the pack. I decide the Indian sends out birds instead of his god—he needs all his gods—and that's why they circle high over me and the girl and the baby. I'm glad the birds don't dive though, putting fear—more of it—into our walk and stumble through the late blue of a long day and then another.

The baby drinks more water at night and eats a crumble of the burnt bread with what grubs I dig up, a good sign for the baby we both agree. We put him between us to sleep, admitting he puts out warmth we need. By morning he's wriggled free and chewing his fist as raw as he can with no real teeth.

I like to think I know where the fort sits on the map, and so does Sharon, who has heard that's where the family was going too if the crops didn't take after their late planting. After a while, we walk on the ruts without covering our steps to go as quick as we can, sharing the baby between us until, like a miracle of where, the fort's timbers glow with lamplight. Then one of the guards shoots at us, being nervous and unused to anyone coming toward the fort in what is now pitch-black. We duck and he shoots again.

I damn him in both Indian and English and I hear something like Bulgarian from the girl. The baby cries because some of the shot missed my head and grazed his bottom. The stupid guard puts his rifle down long enough to hear his cries but almost doesn't open the gates because of the trouble he sees himself suffering from all his fine guarding.

Chapter 7

At least we have our own cell to settle in. At least the baby doesn't die of the shot the way he could have, with all the cell fleas and a flesh wound and no mother. He is used to Sharon more anyway is what I suppose, what with the mother no doubt seeping milk out onto the plow handles whenever she came close enough to wave instead of feed him. At least the fleas here keep him so miserable he couldn't find eternal rest if you laid it in front of him.

He doesn't cry.

My hat lands us in the cell while they consider how we are like spies. Either the hat shows we know someone who doesn't need it in his death or it shows I am all for them. I say I am for shade. In the deep dark of that night with the soldiers taking the horse that I slept on, I couldn't say which side they were for, so I don't tell them about them either. That the baby does not cry makes us more suspicious. But still there is laundry to do. We are released to do laundry whenever they haul water from the river. We are not allowed out of the fort to fetch the water ourselves which I am happy enough with, having fetched plenty of water in the past, and not wanting to meet the Indian, but not being let out at all is not in our plan. For food, the two of us wash their wash and for ourselves we do our own and pin up the baby and think of ways to get out.

The guards have their orders: once in, no out. Weather is coming, and trouble, and we could be part of the trouble. Their captain might let us go if we beg, we are told, except for the weather. Although their captain is not supposed to, he longs to go out and hunt and he travels the river now, in this, the fall time of year, in case Indians have left some game in the low grass. The captain tells everyone he doesn't like to come up short in vittles in winter and that's where they are all headed, into the land of short and cold, with so many mouths open and empty if he doesn't come back soon with this game. Of course, says the guard who taps gunpowder onto the baby's shot hind part to cure it, he, the guard, can't let out the others either.

The others don't eat as much as we do, being sick. We carry water to the sick as a part of what they find for us to do. Many soldiers take sick lounging around and waiting for trouble, in confinement behind the fort's pickets. Some complain of snakebite from snakes slithering out of the fort's walls into their beds, or accidents with hatchets from games they take to playing too hard. One of them shot off his finger pulverizing coffee beans with his revolver. Another five got bit when they provoked a fight between red and black ants to figure which were more courageous. I showed them how to spread a blanket over an anthill so the ants will eat the lice.

Some are actually sick. Two lie wounded from a Kansas skirmish they say they ran from, one with a leftover button still fixed to his rag bandage, wrapped right around his middle where it is blackest with blood. He is a boy my age who likes to sit up in his cot, fever-flushed but pale. He could be both sick and a soldier, wearing a too-big uniform in shoddy, that cheap wool, or else that's all he has to wear.

We soon see a lot of the patients walk out at will to stand at the fire the guard makes, and then close themselves in again at night, so many of them that you know no one wants to recover or escape like us into that soon-to-be real cold outside the fort.

As for the ladies—that's what the guard calls us—we laugh at the jokes the other soldiers tell to get us to come closer. I ask each of them if they have seen a trapper with a big problem of gambling and most of them laugh back, saying that is the trapper's life, a big gamble. Some of them listen closer, hear the rest, about the locket, and the sound of my singing in Bohemian and then they ask more about the four sisters, each of them wearing a different ribbon, they listen and nod and then grab at me when I forget and come close. Let me see your ribbon, they say. When they see I have none, they tease Sharon about hers. That hair afire! they say. It's a wonder you can tie it down at all. Sharon lets them touch her ribbon while I listen to the boy with the bandage talk. Once, he says, he heard of a man drowned from a bet who had a number of daughters, all of them older than he is himself. Then he is red about the ears with the other's catcalls when they notice he is talking to me, then he can't say how many daughters nor what the bet was about so I stop my asking and instead draw on the ground some of my escape plan for Sharon to come upon and add to.

I don't want to stay, food or no food. Not even with the cold. Staying is like working for the Indian all over again. We need to talk to the captain but he is in for hard work and a long trek because in the fall animals love hiding, so fat from grain and roots that all they want to do is hide and sleep. Or else the captain has stepped on some trap of Pa's and can't chop his leg free to tell us.

I don't dwell on the captain's absence. Sharon and I think up escapes instead. Our favorite turns on a wagon train. That the trains set out past here we know, the ruts we followed are laid on into the far horizon. What we want is a return train, we want to be "go-backs," going back for an easy life in a mill town or city so far South that no war will bother it and neither will the cold. Why, a whole train of widows went back last year, says the guard who boasts that he almost married one. Where they were headed Sharon has heard of, the territory called Florida. She says she is not surprised he failed to woo them off the train because if you can manage the fevers some get there, it is real warm year-round.

A fever sounds good to all of us. Everyone knows the cold here can cause craziness, that even the Indians get it—you find their eyes froze shut sometimes, so cold they can't even speak their own talk to make known what happened. I tell Sharon how this is: with any Indian who falls asleep too far from the fire, the ice crawls under his lids and gets at the water in them until he goes blind.

That's hard to believe, she says.

Not as hard to believe as an orange. Have you ever eaten an orange? Florida is where I have heard they grow them.

A man once gave me one, says Sharon. I did not eat it.

She won't say why not.

Summer, summer we bring
Death floats on the stream

Pa knew more words to the tune but they all went with him, I say to Sharon. It is about the season changing, the flash floods, I tell her, plunging my arm into a cold tub of wet laundry.

I don't understand a word, says Sharon. But she seems to. She doesn't grieve over her family or their ways, she doesn't ever sing in Bulgarian.

I tell her Pa is meeting me at a town I know, after I stake a claim.

You are too young to stake a claim, she says.

I can look old if I have to, I say.

Sharon laughs and says no claim is worth looking old for and asks if my Pa is hunting for a wife like all the rest of them. Especially with so many girls.

I am not privy to that, I say. Today is a cold morning, I say.

Winter does promise early, the mice are slow in running, more and more frost climbs the east stockade, flocks turn once overhead and leave, flies cozy up in clumps under any three sticks of wood. Our plan must be nigh. The captain could be dead from the Indians or taken too, with no one returning to tell us.

We allow each other equal time of the baby's heat. The baby doesn't touch ground for another two weeks. He eats what he eats and keeps quiet.

Let me tell you about Harriet, I say while we scrub out the dirt out of four officers' jackets, their chased-off fleas sucking the blood of the baby asleep inside where the wind isn't so cold.

Harriet died, says Sharon. That's what you said. You took her name and what else?

Her real name could have been something else, I say. She told us to call her Harriet in honor of the hair she lost. She lived out a scalping that her people had brought on by their skinning of two Indians first. After she healed up, her father hated looking at her, said her mother looked the same, tortured, bald, and now dead, and he couldn't have her with him even though she could cook and knew poultices. The Indian made a hat of buffalo hair for Harriet and took her as the first to work his snake mound, her being left behind in the prairie by her father.

Like you.

No, I say. I was working off a debt for Pa. That is not the same. And I was there to seek the Indian hoard.

They have a hoard? Sharon laughs.

Pa said. I punch my fist into the soapy coat again and again.

And I reckon you were the lucky sister? Sharon swirls the water with her cold-roughed hand.

My other sisters did not work as hard as I did. I fluster, soap slips into my eyes when I brush my hair away. I tell you what though—I am not going to get into debt with anyone.

That's the ticket, she says. If you can find the route.

The baby cries and I fetch him and stick my short finger into his mouth to keep him from using his new tooth on his own raw one. No point skinning yourself, I say, patting his few short hairs.

Sharon wrings out the last jacket, its brass buttons protruding, row on row. What else about Harriet?

Harriet's mother put mud all over Harriet's head. It didn't work though for the mother.

Sharon nods.

Harriet could plan escapes I heard, I say, but then she died.

That's not our plan, says Sharon.

We lay among the ditches in the dirty yellow mud,
and we never saw an onion, a turnip or a spud

sings the boy over and over. He has the chills until we visit him with a hot cup of some good boiled weeds we have pulled out of our cell cracks. The orchard, I call it, those few shoots still green, and the guard boils them up for us, saying things while feeding the fire like *Rope does not burn unless it's running*. Now that the guard knows us and is suspicious, he is always saying sayings, so many I can't figure out what he means. Don't spoil the eggs, he says, and I don't know if he means Don't plan on fleeing, or Careful, cannonballs are hid close by. I don't want favors of no return from him—this hot cup is our last, I hope, because Sharon has a good plan.

The boy holds the cup away from his chest. I turn hot or cold quick, he says. Like the temper of Jehovah.

You haven't been bad, I say and give the baby up to the ground.

I have seen the elephant, he says.

All the boys say that except the ones on French leave, says Sharon.

I drummed, he says, I drummed on a flat piece of tin so everyone would know to run at each other.

You never said that before, I say.

I was running from it, he says, and lays the cup down as if it's too heavy.

You are too young for drumming any drum, and besides no one fights around here, says Sharon. The war is too far away.

I was in the infantry, he says. He breathes heavy.

Infant-ray. Sound like a baby's thing, I say. We laugh and the baby looks up startled, looks around with just its eyes and then closes them.

You're running a fever. From a wolf bite, maybe, I say. That's it, it's a wolf, not a war you're running from.

The boy shakes his head. He picks up and drinks his drink down, hot or not. I always went first in the fight, he says. It's a danger to go first but they didn't generally take an interest in me because I didn't carry anything to trouble them. Then two did go for me, not wanting to run afoul of the bayonets behind me or the bayonets behind them, two cowards. They teased me away from the others with their own bayonets, took away my drum and talked about war's folly. They treated me kindly, but if anyone asked after me while we ran, I was their prisoner.

You marched all the way here?

They had a horse that we three rode. They planned to take it back where they had land but it took a liking to a she horse all of a sudden and was hard to steer and had to be walked half the time. They walked me right up to within a mile of these gates seeing that I had put in this fever, and then, being unsure of how the wind blew here, sneaked themselves away after I got in. On a horse like that, they probably got knocked off or kicked. They only had a pack.

A black horse? I ask.

I'd say so, he says.

I feel a satisfaction settle in me about that black horse, which must be the same horse I slept on and they stole back. I could run and get the pack to show him right now but an officer would catch me for detail. I pat the boy on one of his hot ears. I wished you could drum us something. Marching is a pleasure if you have a ways to go.

Don't you be thinking of going, says the boy, sitting up on one elbow. There's Indians out there, and nothing. Nothing, not like where I come from, where I did my drumming alongside a man on a trumpet who played real songs.

I was in a tableau where I came from, says Sharon. Every year I did it, I stood in a costume.

That's what it is, living in one place, says the boy. For a while.

I must be like my Pa, I say. I'm always looking for one more surprise in the trap. You never know what you will catch, moving on and on, each a new place, when you trap. I had a doll once that I caught, I say.

Both Sharon and the boy take a look at me. A good doll? asks Sharon.

A doll out of a branch I found.

One of those, says Sharon. But you were too old to keep a doll.

The boy says No, the doll kept her.

Chills make you smart, I say to him. I would never have seen the branch—two legs, two arms and a crooked-handled head—if I had not had been out on the river all day. That's the kind of surprise wandering for traps allows for.

The boy had put on a smile for my story. He relaxes it just then, which is when his color runs out and he slides from a full sit to a lie-down.

We cover him over with his blanket that just about tucks over him. If he is asleep, he can use it. If he isn't, we have heard him.

The bugler plays the only music of the day, which makes Sharon nod slowly as if she feels sorry hearing it. I turn with the baby in a slow, slow dance.

Chapter 8

Before the pumpkin moon, we escape.

Chapter 9

We plod forward into the cloudiness, faces bent to our feet, hearing only the hard wind at our ears which ratchets even bird noise low, when a darker shade covers us. We walk quite a ways under its dim pitch without noticing—why would we, breathing so hard?—its whooshing or the very regular shape of its coming and going. Only a shot makes us look up, and the man's cry.

Oh my beautiful balloon! The man's waving a monocle in a crazy *z*, the large canvas sphere overhead with flame in it plunging and whistling backwards at a wild speed, a gun and another man dangling from its basket. *Dumkopf!* screams the monocled man.

I run backwards, agog, sure I will fall on the baby strapped to my back.

Sharon is stopped and gaping.

Fire crawls over the balloon as the basket plunges. What little silk is left aloft arrests this plunge so that the balloon comes down in small huffs, and where it lands is not far from where I am running, both forward and backward in avoidance, and only the basket is not spurting flame.

The two men leap out of it, each hauling a sack of sand that they empty over the silk fire.

Enough of the silk is saved, though some of its red is singed to brown lace. One of the men scrounges in the lacy shambles for his dropped monocle, which he then shakes at the sun as if the sun itself has betrayed him. The other man runs his hand through his hair, his opposite hand still gripping his gun. *Mein hassenfeffer*, he says with disappointment.

You drunken *dumkopf!* shouts the man with the monocle. I shot the rabbit, he says, with such seriousness.

The baby cries. So quiet all along, though surely he has hunger with all its difficult gnawing, so quiet even while the gun shoots and flames lick the silk, he cries only after the basket hits the ground. It's strange he cries at all, he so seldom does, and his cry is strange too, it would have been a word if he knew one but no matter, the sound stops me as surely as the shot coming from above, which could have been thunder. This is prairie, after all, weather is anything from anywhere.

Oh, baby, I say to him, pulling him to my front.

The cursing, the hullaballoo, the stomping around of the two saved-by-their-skin men does not compete with his bawling. His body goes stiff and he cries even louder. I hold him away from me, he's like a length of wood with thrashing arms, I turn him—what else?—until he stops weeping. His distant wild look as he sobs makes me turn to it. I drag both of us a few feet further into his gaze and there, in amidst the brush, lies a fallen sausage.

I grope between the dry pricks of the prairie grass and out it comes, and just as quick my knife. I have only to raise the sausage toward Sharon to jolt her out of her balloon-staring and join us. The three of us eat slices in as silent a jubilance as starvation can command, we devour a good bit of that sausage, all in a huddle, while those men wander and lament and curse and blame, shouting in languages I can't quite hear over my chewing. Then the man with the monocle and so many buttons down his front that it's a field of tiny shields, swears in words I know well, from my father and his rages.

It makes me happy to hear something so fatherly, I tell Sharon who glances up from the sausage she's slicing into circles and smiles her first real smile at the sound of him.

The baby sucks and drools onto his meat, the tears from his crying salting his slices. I put by some of the sausage for him, we don't eat it all, though it all disappears before the man with the buttons can stride over on stiff legs to turn his glassy monocle to us. Good day, he says, as if he has just been lowered quietly on a cloud.

Sharon and I nod. We would have nodded to *I am a god*.

In English, though with such an accent, he asks into what acreage have they fallen and, more or less, which way out and where are we headed with one of us wearing a cap like that.

A fort, I lie. Why trust people who fall out of the sky? My true path is still Pa's, east and east only. Yonder, I gesture to where the horizon is met by the river, opposite to where we left the fort behind.

Ah, yes, he says. Of course. He flaps a wine-stained map, its rivers and lakes dripping and disappearing.

Sharon reties her ribbon.

He thanks us, bowing slightly as if his back hurts to bow for anyone but perhaps it does hurt from his landing, and then he commands his helper, he calls him Lieutenant *Dumkopf*, to clean the sand sack so he can fill it with his traveling materials, his books, his cloaks, and his spyglass if it be spared by their inopportune landing, as he calls it.

To see the dregs of sand emptied to the wind by the lieutenant—sand to me an especial burden—and ordered emptied by a man so willful, a man quite Pa-like, with at least some love of gaming in him, proven by this now-withered vast gamble of a balloon once aloft and now fallen—and to hear our shared tongue, why, all of this dizzies me. My memory of Bohemia, what's left of it or what's secondhand from stories from my sisters or Pa himself, is peasant furrows running right to its lack of a seaport surrounded by happy-to-exploit-you powers with no real borders, water or mountain. It is not that I trust this man now for this sum of his Pa-ness or even by virtue of his accent, but I do appreciate how they come together, especially the curses which my father, who wanted his girls to learn everything in this new language of English, translated all of: the cock's big crow, the scrotum of the adder's mother-in-law, your grape-sized brain.

Not bad, when put against the peddler's curses.

Then the lieutenant curses too, he weaves doing it but while smiling the smile of a wine guzzler, a stain of the same in an arabesque across his uniformed chest. By way of introduction, he tells us in half English that his own daughters insist he is no one, like all fathers, that they are girls who pluck at their hems and pretend instead to be ladies-in-waiting for anybody's royalty and ignore him. The girls who don't ignore him are the wine girls. He smiles at us bigger. It is clear that what he really likes is the wine, not the girls. Lieutenant *Dumkopf!* He is told to bundle all of the this and the that, and not to forget the water cask. All the empty wine bottles he is ordered to leave behind, despite the way he lifts them and looks into them, along with so much of the rope, and a candelabra.

Leave something so bird-necked and curious as a silver candelabra?

While Sharon and I circle it, the lieutenant heaves the burnt basket to, and out of its bottom he pulls down wheels, very light but wide, which turns the basket into a barrow. He then loads it with the bundles and all the shredded once blood-red silk, every slip of it. He does not however leave the great mass of tangled rope, no matter what the button-shielded superior's order, but he does leave that great-necked candelabra at a tilt on the dirt.

We touch the candelabra, fingers at either end.

I am a prince, says the monocled man, his throat-clearing a grating drumroll. He puts this forth in accented English, and not in the language of his curses. Prince von Hoffenbaum, he adds. He lifts one of his hands as if to suggest our kissing it, as if to suggest his whole Bohemian princedom, its distant but fertile lands, its very clouds. We suffer this introduction and present curtsies, lifting our torn hems. The names we offer for ourselves he inclines his head slightly after. The baby continues his new quiet, sucking a triangle of sausage invisibly, gumming it as he would.

My balloon and its works are in the employ of this country, he says. I make miraculous reconnaissance of enemy progress every day, for one side or the other. This day or the day before—it matters not—a storm took us from our bounden duty and we were forced to consume the bulk of our rations.

This is when I notice he too weaves slightly.

We are in the midst of a long travail, Sharon volunteers.

I see, he says. He makes a note with his pencil in a journal he produces from his pocket. Surely he understands what she's said as *trail*, because he then insists we lead them in our former direction. The lieutenant, tossing out the broken sextant and a pot, does not venture anything otherwise. I reflect that the two of them could offer a kind of rough protection for us and I re-shoulder the baby. Sharon throttles the candelabra and takes up our pack behind me. The lieutenant mostly pulls the barrow, though sometimes it is caught and saved from a slight downhill hurry by all of us, even the prince, in fear of both losing or being crushed by his necessities.

Thus it is that they follow us into the ruts beside the river, away from the fort.

It is no use discussing any other route anyway, with nowhere else in the whole wide vista to aim for, unless it be the two buffalo and their calves in the eye-watering distance—but all three of those could just be trees. However, after enough hours have gone that the sun has almost sunk and any hint of trees have been walked past, the prince embarks on a chat in English about direction, their own, as if our own lies that much adjacent, and on discovering the looseness upon which we are progressing and the fort at our backs, he suggests, no, he prays that we all stop at once and make camp.

You have led me astray, says the prince, pointing at a dip in the flat land behind us. We shall have to find a new way. His monocle falls off his face in emphasis and swings on a loop pinned to his chest. I should have you arrested

A rest! I agree, says his lieutenant, coming up behind him, catching the monocle. I think we should rest.

The prince groans. But the fire is struck anyway and a portion of the prince's remaining rations are shared out, more or less, in princely, that is, in monarchical style, with the prince getting the best and the most, and the rest of us receiving our shares with thankful postures, saying nothing about his foolishness in following us, nor about any arrest. Any further threats are lost in the ensuing desuetude of our location, while the prince surveys the empty distant ruts—*Where could those supply wagons be now?*—pressing his monocle against his broken spyglass. In that interlude Sharon starts up in a voice a tableau anywhere might require: We tore the dead boy's blanket into strips then braided it the way you would a hunk of hair.

Really? says the prince, perusing the rivers of wine stain on his map.

I put the baby over the fence first, in case of wolves, she says.

She strikes a pose and howls.

The prince abandons his survey. The lieutenant sits up. I am handling the baby and nearly drop him.

How would we know if wolves were there, otherwise? she says. If they showed, we would have hoisted him back in. Harriet had already fixed up some other idea. Harriet knows about wolves.

I nod when they turn to me. But tossing the baby over first was a surprise tack to me too. I start to say how we planned it but Sharon says, Quiet.

The baby makes a noise so we know he hits the ground, she says. We use the rise the bugler's grave gives near the wall, just enough, she says, so the baby can't be hurt too bad. No wolves come that night, it's too dark and they like the moon better, or maybe something likes them too in dark like that. No one in the fort comes out when the baby cries. They are used to his cries.

She makes her own little cry and moves her hands in the shadow of the fire against the basket so the prince can see it's us in the fort.

This is our story, I say, by way of explaining. Pretty much.

She says the soldiers are all playing cards for stakes. One of them had rendered tallow from bear grease that afternoon and they had piles of soap to bet with, and the only guards stood at the front and the back.

We saw Southerners the night of the storm, the prince interrupts, perhaps the very night you speak of. Running for the withers of their grey-coated fathers, seeing our basket hanging over them in the dark sky. Albert so-and-so, we could hear them calling, we were that close. I do not know any Alberts, he says. A general perhaps.

He produces a candle for the candelabra. Light? he says in Bohemian to the lieutenant.

The lieutenant lights the candle with a brand rolled from the fire.

Sharon continues her talk with as many tableau effects her voice and limbs allow. The prince interrupts with a speech about Civil War this and the Civil War that, so many battles he surely has not witnessed but can guess, having the left-behind Prussian front to fall back on, the cavalry cutting off foot soldiers being identical anywhere. They could have both been telling the same story, speaking as they were back and forth, gesturing at the fire, making shadows that stab.

Wild creatures creep close but no closer with our fire kept high by the lieutenant who trembles from the lack of wine he mentions in a whisper once and then again, with no apparent answer from the prince who speaks as fast as Sharon in a kind of competition, while closing and opening his monocled eye and peering at the sleeping baby which, he says, drawing a breath, could be almost a match to one he had once fathered in an afternoon's folly with a serving maid who had the audacity to produce it from a basket of laundry and hold it up next to him while his mother reminded her that all babies resemble him in features—the long forehead, the small mouth. Sharon does pause to laugh, then continues relating every detail of our travail, from the lightning-struck family to the red cloud of a balloon scudding across the sky that made our walk so darkly shadowed—but says nothing about herself, I am the daughter of such and such from this town, no, nothing so mundane and previous as that, no, she relates only our adventure until all of it is released and settles, light ash, onto our open-mouthed snoring.

Chapter 10

Bottles, says the prince, his hand outstretched in demand.

Bottles? repeats the lieutenant. More bottles? More wine? A smile alights on his lips, pulls up one side.

The other bottles, hisses the prince. Listening to you clank forward, I am drawn to wondering what has become of the other bottles.

It is as much as the tenth tuffet of brush the lieutenant has met in a mile that arrests him in exhaustion as it is the prince's hiss. Why—aren't they in their hidey-hole?

The prince kisses the air at his lieutenant's insouciance. Yes, yes, they must be. But I am asking you to fetch them for me.

The lieutenant wrestles the silk to the walls of the basket and rummages in it, hanging over the inside—rope, burnt silk, the monocle case—no! Then he climbs right into the basket to rummage some more, his backside alert in its search. What he at last produces is six small flagons strapped to each other on a leather belt. Blue-glassed and squat with derby-shaped droppers, one is opened by the prince, who lets fall a little into his mouth. He hates it, he says, pointing the dropper toward the lieutenant. Not schnapps.

The lieutenant, so sober, frowns.

We pick up our feet. A peddler told me about this bottle, I say to Sharon when the prince is enough ahead. Inside it is an animal that throws itself on you and sucks your breath away until you dream crazy. The peddler gave the Indian cat piss instead of this drug the Indian had ordered, for himself and for me, and the Indian had him beaten for the wrong dreams.

The bottles are so blue, Sharon rasps in her used-up voice from the night before. I do like blue, she calls to the prince, who turns.

Add a sneeze of gold in the foundry and *Voila!* red, the prince says. I am so happy—none of them are broken. My supply comes from the front and you never know how close to go.

Wine, says the lieutenant.

Ether is even easier. If there were ether inside these bottles we could throw them into a buffalo herd and collect the animals that drop. Just one buffalo would do, he says, looking out at the flatness now devoid of anything—like his eyes. Or just one deer.

A colder wind blows up. Walking forward, no one says anything more about the bottles or game, especially not the prince, who keeps quaffing from the dropper then taking very long strides we have to run to keep up with. Another big gust blows, with a few flakes. Sharon announces that winter would have had us at the fort. She sounds, in her tone, like she is warming up—for a new talk.

Pa hated visiting forts, I say, quick before she can go on. They taxed the traps and such. Once he bought flour at a fort in exchange for two months' worth of skins, and they kept his hat for the tax. Or so he said when he came back hatless and nearly earless with only that flour in a sack. Or, I suppose, thinking about it, it could have been a bet.

I can talk too and I do, until the prince says, Stop here. The bottle he carries he squints at and shakes, then refits it empty into its holster of others.

The lieutenant says his own *Yes* in Bohemian, a *Dah* of great exhaustion. Feeling such hunger too, *Dah*, even the prince's hunger, but feeling his thirst even more, he says he is dying of thirst—for his wine, something real to drink other than river water, he tells us as he lays the cart on its side against the ground, flops down in its little shade near the sleeping baby, lies with his head on his arm and licks his lips for their bloody saltiness, and rants.

Ach, your bottles, he says to the resting prince who rolls his moon-sized eyes at his moaning. Oh, for his girls and their sweet sticky fingers, their pastries and thick jams, their thieving the vineyards for bunches he could crush with his feet and prepare properly—which of his girls is turning his bottles? The bottles will all go off, all of a splendid season, a whole year's worth of wine. He should have married one of their mothers, he should have looked in his socks for money to keep them to turn his wine. But at least he himself is not gone off. That is it, he is not shot as yet, the way so many others of his lot were lined up to be shot in the homeland, or drilling to be shot day after day. No, he dangled from a balloon, God willing, and then fallen, is here, in the land of the freed man—*Svoboda!*—he is as yet not quite dead.

He sleeps.

The prince decrees a new direction determined from the sun and the wind, a royal wind he has declared it, he's snobby about wind too, it is his wind, the balloon's, we will all go that way, his supplies will arrive there. He's teetery after all his droppers but bold—he admonishes us to leave the river, to march far away from it. There is another river, a better one I remember from being aloft. Lift your legs to your chin, he says, it will loosen the stiffness, and the wind will help you.

We beg to disagree. I am inclined not to change rivers but he does not care where we are inclined, even the baby's thirst does not matter to him. If we had archers, they would shoot ahead of us, but we have no archers, he says. This land provides no landmarks, he says. Only from above you can see, if there is anything to see, he complains.

We set off in a crazy-march, the sleepy lieutenant hauling the basket behind us into the wilds of the brush. After some time spent pressing into his vista, the prince peers out of the grass beside us as if we ourselves are game, checking our progress with his, and demands that we hug his route closer. Sharon swerves as he wishes, and I veer slowly and follow, baby tight to my back, his seat on my cupped hands.

When the sun descends low enough, I pry the baby off my shoulder where he now sucks at my clothes, I lay the baby down. I feel finished, utterly finished, with our travels, travails, the trail. I do not care where the prince is walking, he can walk right onto the moon if he wants. Sharon sinks down beside me, loosening her pack and setting the candelabra down. Weary with laugh-on-a-bump, weary with worry over the baby's thinness, the milky white sheen of him tight to his bone, his little waste, I lay him on my shin. Horsey, I say to him and I bounce him on my leg until he burps and grins like any baby.

The lieutenant has fallen far behind in detour. Clumps

of wild rye and broom and spurge that spring up wherever buffalo have been obstruct him. When there's a rise, he tugs the basket forward to where it rattles down slow, on its own weight. Coming upon us at last with a halt and a crash, the lieutenant spits.

The lieutenant says he has spit most of the day. From the dryness, he explains. You will be that dry too someday, he grins. From wine. He frowns. He has kept half an eye on us the whole time, surveying us even while we relieved ourselves most modestly, then backing off in rattling mayhem when the prince called him forward. It is a kind of measuring, his watching, as if he's figuring how much wine are we worth.

A shave, the prince interrupts his spitting with his command. He has been tapping his monocle to his chin, marking the spot of our collapse, waiting for him and his basket. This is the sort of thing a body must attend to, says the prince, or you are lost for good.

His monocle falls into his hand in preparation.

The lieutenant mutters more about *Svoboda* but produces a kit, decants water from a canteen we all guzzle from a cup, then strops a razor by the waning light.

We are hungry again, says Sharon, who talks for us both I am so tired.

Mon Dieu, says the prince, perhaps more in fear of her going on than of the lieutenant's razor slips or even of hunger. The supplies are not yet refreshed as you can well see. Although—he says, and he lifts his head to the horizon, his chin just missing the lieutenant's knife—I expect them soon. My associates will find us taking this route.

The lieutenant lifts a brow, his implement raised.

We do expect them, the prince repeats.

I could shoot, I say. I saw game as we walked. I have checked the traps of my father. I chose this spot because I know where animals might drink this time of day, and later.

The lieutenant appraises me.

Poacher, the prince says with the great disdain of his class and the often fed, not with his true soul that could yet be born, the one that aches from foraging, the one that learns too well the hard art of pilfer and beg.

The lieutenant shaves around his long mustache.

I am skillful with my father's whistle and can call the thrush, a deer or a moose, I tell him. What I learned from Pa is that an animal will surely pay us notice hearing it, and most probably a visit. Or we can attach a ball of wicking soaked with kerosene to the tail of a turtle and tuck it into a hole to smoke out a woodchuck. If you have wicking and kerosene. Or we can teach an otter to catch fish for us, if we have the time and ever find this new river.

The prince pauses to consider my offer.

Sharon twists her ribbon in loops.

Lieutenant, he says. Search the basket again.

With alacrity and sureness he produces another sausage, his face after this effort just as red as its withered casing. The prince accepts it, gives out what little he must, his knife in his fist wielding most un-prince-like in division. We eat every scrap quick, the last stub of our own sausage shared out in secret the day before.

We will hunt together, announces the lieutenant, licking his lips. I can help, he says, in his most fatherly fashion. He remembers a buffalo chip he thought he saw somewhere, he says. We could creep up on them.

No, I say. I roll the dirt on my palm out of its cracks. What if the wind goes wrong?

Sharon is sidling up to the prince as if she knows which way the wind will blow.

While I march off to flush some game with the lieutenant and his gun, I dwell on why Sharon refused that orange she spoke of in the fort. What more forbidden fruit in the prairie is there than the orange, its juice in runnels to the wrist, and no way to cover up the scent of it, caught on every touch, every breath? Opening an orange in a closed room at night would start plenty—if nothing else, talk. It does happen that girls flee talk by signing on to a wagon train, or some of those girls get themselves into trouble in the desperation of the journey and then spend their confinement in a room over the first saloon they reach. A girl could swell as she crossed the plains, denying the swelling, saying she was putting on pounds, saying she was too young, that she knew no one—and knowing none of the weeds that work.

Sharon could pose in tableau, after an orange.

Out of the tallest grass, I flush a wild cow and its calf gone astray from one of those wagon trains. I convince the lieutenant not to shoot the mother. It will pull the basket, I tell him. The lieutenant isn't so sure the cow has it in her to take the harness but does allow me to trick it into giving milk for the thin baby's supper. Then he shoots the calf and holds the baby while I truss it to the gun. It was a good calf. It stood beside the mother and did not run. I carry it back while he leads the mother.

The prince soon directs the lieutenant's turning of the carcass over a small blaze, the prince being, as he takes pains to repeat, also an expert with fire, its keeping and its snuffing, both on land and in the air.

Instead of taking a pose near the glories of the dripping

roasting meat, Sharon questions the prince, standing close to him to ask with seriousness such things like *How, with regard to the air, does the balloon rise?*

The prince pokes his finger into the dust beside the fire to show her, he outlines all of its processes with stones and pinches of dust, and she does not look into the fire for relief from these long careful answers but moves closer to him to ask him even more: *What paste secures the silk? How high float the level clouds?* She does not ever ask about spirits dancing in the sky, or about hearing angelic music at that height. He compliments her for this, saying all conveyors of balloons and their contraptions suffer incessantly from such stupid queries. Since only his birth, intellect, and economic position separate the two of them—and they are well united in his taste for adoration—he begins to enjoy himself. He commandeers the turning of the calf, his fresh-shaved face shining with vigor while the lieutenant constructs a harness to join the cow to the basket.

He is the devil, I say to the baby. Fallen out of the sky like that, with a devil's moustache and the sound of the talk of my own people! And taking us away from the river. That's how I know the devil's come for us especially. Oh, you—don't cry, don't cry, I won't make another face. Shshshsh. Just this.

I cross myself the way the Indians do. The devil doesn't notice, he is pointing out ash floating over the embers, explaining the work of air.

From up in a balloon you can see quite a bit, I interrupt just when he's getting serious about hot and cold valences, what he calls the winds.

Not everyone is allowed to look over the side, says the prince, his monocle winking in reflected light like a one-eyed devil. Some, he says, can't look down at all. A certain nausea overcomes them seeing the ground for the first time as it moves underfoot while the balloon weighs toward the tops of trees and the undulating bird flight. It is a regal view from a balloon, so few can tolerate it. But your eye owns every human on the road, cows, cannon—

The prince spreads his arms in princely fashion, owning it all.

My Pa traps, I say. If you had seen him walking below—

I have seen many people on foot and horseback, says the prince. We once saw an animal show from above, with elephants as small as—by what name are they known? He addresses the lieutenant who is trying the harness on himself.

Ants, says his lieutenant. He confirms the word as if it were cutlery or fresh socks, not as if he knows something more than the prince.

Mice, says the prince.

I have never seen an elephant, I say.

Instead of admitting anything, Sharon raises her arm to her face like an elephant's trunk. The shadow of her arm against the basket dangles. We laugh when she flails it and waves it, and the prince's mustache actually wriggles in what could be mirth. Very theatrical, he says.

Pa wears a beaver hat, I say, as patient as ever. Maybe you could see it from up there.

They are just the fashion, says the prince.

I suppose there are others with beaver hats, I say. But Pa has with him three daughters all almost grown by now, probably dressed in gingham because that's what the oldest liked best. They pulled his wagon sometimes too, if the horse went lame or he lost it in a bet.

I have seen that, says the lieutenant. He is dreaming, half-lidded, beside the fire, enjoying the downwind heat of the roasting, the harness resting on his chest.

In the morning, says the prince, the valences pull this way—he leans toward Sharon.

The dung chips burn white and whiter. The prince breaks his talk to administer to himself with his dropper, thus the lieutenant takes over the spit. He goes on himself in a pretend prince voice, saying, There are no decent trees here. The heavy-boughed orchards at home, the smell of burnt cherry wood, the birds circling, the sweet fruit, a chill night, a good wine—

Does he speak English? Does he speak Bohemian? We talk of orchards, their remembered redolence, of spread branches and old world darkness, as much of the darkness as anyone remembers.

In the midst of this sigh of ours, the prince produces a box of salt and admonishes the lieutenant to carve the meat.

The prince is pleased with his piece.

Sucking on a bone, Sharon says, I'm thinking of getting married in a beaver hat.

We turn to her, our fingers slick with grease. That is an idea, I say.

She is hardly ready for marriage. Her chest harbors just a nip of breast but they're really nothing against her skinniness, her eyes are fastened so loose that if they see you in some lights, you aren't sure they are separate from each other. She has one crooked finger and her hair holds only that old ribbon.

She is pretty enough when she poses.

The lieutenant breaks the longest bones for the baby to

suck, then picks out a piece of calf fat to polish the prince's boots. He does not jerk the fat across them but pets the leather with it, pets the boots in smooth circles we watch in what firelight is left. Then the prince goes out into the dark on some personal errand as he puts it and the lieutenant follows along after.

You see, says Sharon, if I say I am ready for marriage, they will want to safeguard me.

I say no, quite the opposite, but she starts speaking again before she can hear my answer, and I wonder whether we met during a dry spell of her going on and on. She is wondering now about ants, whether they toil by night, and at the suddenness of the dead boy-drummer's dropping off and if he had the cholera too, and at the dumbness of the baby. My head hurts with all her wondering talk, I want to sleep.

The prince returns with the lieutenant, arms on shoulders, all smiles. The lieutenant removes the prince's boots, *Umph*, *Umph*, and sets them, two sentries, at the edge of the fire.

I hold a stick into the shadows so it points away from the balloonists, away from now, into a future Sharon can't see. What can the stick tell me? You would think the dark is death or at least the unborn or unthought, but no, to me it is the future, what I don't know. But I see that Sharon wants to know it now, she is talking it up for herself when she says to the yawning prince, Do you sing?

I put the stick down.

Chapter 11

Gunfire and smoke mark a spot two rises ahead, past where the river returns near the base of a single tree as the river were looking for it.

Perhaps patchwork could be had there, says the prince, anywhere it is worth shooting. It is not necessarily the enemy winning, he adds.

They might be, says the lieutenant. He hopes for a drink either way, a drink on the way to prison or a toast to their spying. Just one more. The lieutenant steps lively past the frowning prince and doesn't stop like we do until the prince calls him back, then it is hard for him to get exactly back. The cow does not pull straight, then it does, and he has to move wherever it goes.

If nothing else, people set against each other have supplies, says the prince.

We stop at that tree to roast and divide a snake I snared for noon supper, and drink up the last of the lovely almost-spritz the prince kept in his pocket flask, then we fill it with new river water.

We need a volunteer to tell us who is winning, says Sharon. Someone to go first.

A scout, I say in the silence.

The lieutenant unfolds himself flat to the ground so the prince sees less of him. He will collect the supplies, says the prince. If they are found.

Sharon is working ash against her teeth for shine, and spitting.

I am looking for my Pa, I say. Something—

I sit up on my haunches, scan the emptiness behind me, the discharge of cannon so far ahead in the distance, smoke—I remember the tree, but there wasn't any town—

Towns are made on the morrow. They could indeed have dry goods, says the prince. He puts the spyglass to his monocle. The river makes an oxbow down there at the first house.

You can take the baby, Sharon says. Surely there will be a place for orphans in a village worth fighting over.

It could be Indians besetting, I say.

With cannon redoubt? asks the prince. He polishes his monocle and resets it on his eye socket. Unlikely. The smoke seems diminished already, he says.

You're the one always wanting to leave the baby, I say to Sharon. He is your kin.

Did I say he is related to me? She pulls herself up straight. The girls and the family, yes.

I don't remember exactly, I say slow, waiting for her to remember better.

But she doesn't. You are in charge of him now, she says. But then she says—looking away—he likes to sleep sucking on something. See that he has something. And boil a corncob now and then for sweetness. He may like that too.

Yes, I will see to it, I say.

Upon your return, the lieutenant will locate their supply

of silk, commandeer provisions, and obtain the secret whereabouts of the enemy or even of a few of these bottles, then I will sew the balloon tight enough to build a fire under it and all of us sail away and search for your Pa, says the prince, and then we will find him from our high position above the land. If he is not in the town already, adds the prince. The prince offers me the final link of the cooked snake.

Sharon fastens the baby to my back. He appears to be getting longer, his legs dangling halfway down, his head almost touching mine, his few sprouts of head hair tickling my neck. The prince announces that I am just a girl with a baby, nobody will bother me. No need to even trouble with farewells, he says. You will return soon enough.

Without the baby, says Sharon, you can search for your Pa more quickly.

Sharon and the prince are bent over the two last blue bottles when I look back, they are bent low and close.

No sentries stand where they would, at the front end of the twenty-house town, just two dogs are tied to a post so they won't run off at the sound of gunfire. They bark and bark and pull at their rope tied tight, they bark but they have been barking since before I walked close to them.

I swing the baby off my back and sit beside the dogs in what sun is left, half the day gone in getting there. When the baby starts to wriggle his hands in the air, in that lonely way of his, I press him to me.

I'm sure he knows, like dogs do, that leaving him is part of why we're here. I cry a little over that left feeling I know so well that I even hate to hear about it. Or else I'm tired.

But you can't cry for too long in a place where people are

groaning all around. Blue groans or grey? I wipe the tears off my face with my cap and wonder what side I should be from. The hat's of a color that doesn't tell anything other than it's from fighting or bad dyeing. One of the dogs sniffs at it as if he will eat it so I leave it for him.

Come on, baby, I tell him to his sad face. Let's find a home for you.

The first dead man lies at the town pump and I have to pull him away to get at the water. I go ahead and drink anyway. I damp-wash the baby in the trough below the pump and give him my finger to quiet him. Might as well be a clean given-away baby, though the water is winter cold. Already wet myself, I pump and swing under the handle at the same time for my own cold rinse, with the cold baby flailing and crying at the water that wets him again, lying flat to the ground.

Whoever wants, can shoot us or not.

I drag myself and the baby through the whole length of the town, all burnt wood and broken bottles, except for one whole pane of unbroken window glass that leans against a wall. No live person comes out from his house to greet me, there's just groans. I head toward a store at the other end where provisions should lie but I don't go right in, I loiter behind a barrel that's leaking slow from a bullethole. It's too quiet.

A man in a soldier jacket pushes out the door and backheels his way down the steps laden with crackerboxes, a ham haunch, and a bottle, and the shopkeeper follows him. The man runs off down the street, items slipping. The shopkeeper kneels and takes aim with a gun, he blasts away at the fleeing ham haunch but in between one of those angry blasts that don't hit a thing, someone else shoots the shopkeeper from another angle. Wounded, he staggers a step forward with his smoking gun, looks down at the red spreading from his apron side, moves off from his door and falls down his step, not far from where I am in observance.

Whoever shot him could see me, and he could still be there, watching that apron get red to its hem. I must run off but I can't. Someone else shoots from somewhere else and, instead of running, I tuck that baby down and pick my way around the shopkeeper, up the step and inside the store quick, to hide under a shelf and shake for a long while. Someone whose shot goes right through the shopkeeper could find it in himself to trouble a girl and a baby. But maybe that last shot I heard got him.

I hug the baby to me and he belches foully.

A laugh comes out of me then, as short and hard as that belch, but a laugh. I rise up to set the baby on the counter and locate a sugar treat. He eats it in his usual silence. I catch him a pickle from a barrel but he won't have it. Fussy, I say to him like a scold. I suck the salt juice off the pickle then I eat the pickle myself. I see calico and sacking all around me, I see the gingham my sisters favor over the softest hides of animals, and in a far corner, behind a stack of machine-made crackers, a bolt of dress silk. A gauzy green.

I lay a length of it over my arm, then over my shoulders. The baby has crawled to the jerky and is eating it, sucking at its toughness, not minding me when I try to get him to touch the silk.

The dogs stop their barking. Someone let them go?

In that silence and strain, I succumb to a lie-down on a length of worsted behind the cash drawer that the baby sighs into, still holding a salt cracker he has found upright between his fingers. Chilled from our pump bath or all those threats of a shooting, we shiver and listen close to the silence for so long I fall dead asleep and dream I'm back with the Indian.

It is a waltz the Indian wants us to do that William the Hat has taught him, with hip dips and side steps and held out arms. We girls have never seen a waltz done—I saw it at the fort later—and nothing, William nor the Indian dancing with William, makes it look more like a dance than any of the others. We take our positions anyway, one across from the other, stamping the steps the way we always do, the music the usual bells at our ankles and drumming. Waltz, William calls out again. Then, like dreams will, I see from above all of us dancing, with the wind tearing at us and the dust in it, and the wheat I sowed growing green up the side of a long mound that bends like a snake twice, a snake with an open mouth that William, the doubled girls, the Indian with his foot raised, and the baby—the baby's in the dream too—all waltz toward.

Or else the mound-snake is coming for them.

The baby cries. I wake from that high-up-view dream—a balloon's—and there the baby is, his eyes open. I've only slept a minute and he none. He's watching me with his pale eyes. It isn't exactly comfort they give, it is more as if there is a dog that guards, the kind that knows a snake's intentions. Or like a lamp. He is always lit.

Chapter 12

I locate another bolt of silk for the balloon, and am tying one to the other with rope when a woman enters with a white-hatted servant, both wild in their eyes from stepping over the shopkeeper where he is being ministered to at last, they say, by two others. They skitter but do not shriek, they look as if they are all shrieked out. I want two yards, says the woman as soon as I get to the counter. I need—her eyes take in the silk I am holding as wrong—two yards of muslin rag. We have wounds to bind.

I can measure and do, I am deft with a scissors, I cut.

The little monkey, says the woman's servant to the baby as if this were an animal she saw everyday. Those quick hands. She points to his grip over the few coins they offer.

Soon others crowd in with more wounds to bind. I unbolt as much as they want and charge as little as they have. I give away three yards for a dead child and a bolt end for a doll that got shot. Black is for later. Someone arranges for the shopkeeper's burial and I cut six yards of plaid for him, exclaiming it was his favorite. In the midst of all this wound-binding and scissoring and terror, I find my face curling up into a smile.

After all the searching and shopkeeping and then the finding of a "simple jar of honey" for a young sulfur-smelling man with a terrible headache from exploding powder who dies on the shop step just after I sell him the jar, I do not want to leave this shop's sudden safety—except to tell Sharon this is no place to leave a baby, a place so full of confoundment. After all, it is her baby, at least a baby she had first.

When the night comes in as black as shot, I shake myself out of this safety. I close the shop tight and carry the baby and the silk and a box of crackers and jerky through the black streets where no lamps at all are lit, there's just the groans of the still dying or of the getting better that follow me from inside their houses, more groans than before, as if only now can they let them out. I walk into the dark at the edge of town where the brush thickens and the houses end and the road loses its ruts, past the pump where we washed, I walk into the dark toward that tree where the others should be with Sharon, where I left them.

The moon keeps finding clouds. Soon I'm not entirely sure which way and where. I walk through wheat stubble, cold-scuffed thistle and bent-over grass, I turn at where dust wisps around and stop.

Nothing of the balloon or its people casts the slightest shadow in any of the directions in the dark's day-like bursts of moon.

I can't find them.

Maybe it's because I've brought the baby. I wasn't supposed to bring him back. Maybe I shouldn't, after that dream I had.

I haul the baby and the food and the silk here and there until the moon sinks half down in its clouds. Once I spot a bent bush and then a track that could be deep from supplies but it leads to dust. Did they wade to the other side of the river to eat all the rest of the rations without me? Did Sharon offer her skirt and the lieutenant his breeches to patch the silk? Did the prince's associates find them with their supplies? They are gone so completely into the dark prairie with their big basket of burst balloon it is as if they have impossibly risen away from it. I consider the dark chill water and how short a time they put by to wait for me.

The silver candelabra glitters against a bush. Sharon must've heard a promise better than such a candelabra to leave it. I sit down beside it, in the dirt. I consider hauling the baby and myself after them on land, going on to look for them the way I spent time looking for Pa, but the baby is heavy, heavier even without his eating much, the baby is almost a child. But I could leave the baby. While I do my considering, a boiling anger gets me to my feet.

We have been left.

I take the candelabra back to the shop to remind myself the baby didn't fall from the sky, nor is really my brother. To prove we are the shopkeeper's kin, I wrap a length of plaid around the baby the same as the one I chose for the shopkeeper's laying out. The next day just a few of the townspeople come in. They have their services to attend to, and the shopkeeper had just settled in a month earlier, they tell me, with a wagon of fresh ginghams and thick wools and silk—and me, I remind them, who arrived the day of the fight, his niece. He was my uncle, didn't he tell you? And this is my orphan cousin, I explain for the baby, and we both cry hard at the service when it's the shopkeeper's turn. I have plenty to cry about, but I say nothing anyone could undercut with intent.

It is just about winter, after all.

The general store I occupy is situated two hundred paces or so from the river where it turns its oxbow against a small bluff, with a door out back for kitchen work, a front door, and a step up for customers. A nice store, it is not so close to the other part of town, but who knows which way the town will go? People have staked off their squares and cattycorners for commerce in all directions, and the start of a boardwalk is coming my way.

A week after the shopkeeper's funeral, I move the counter—just a board over barrels—so I can keep an eye on what street there is for Pa. I set aside some silk for my sisters. I don't discount that in the past he could have traveled here alone or even with me and my sisters. There were so many settlements puny and one-horse, there were so many that sprouted streets and wells or disappeared. Even forts went out of business from one trapping trip to the next.

For months townspeople show up in a dazed and shrill state to argue—not about my presence behind the counter—but about which side shot them up. The men who rode in, Jayhawkers for sure, did not cry, *Preserve the Union!* nor anything from Dixie. They just plain looted, that was it. I nod, recalling my own Jayhawkers with their black horse and drummer boy. Varmints and renegades, they say, taking full advantage of an excess of government-issued uniform parts. They chew tobacco I offer out that they pay for, spitting into my spittoon, a damp bucket. Why, the varmints were lucky we didn't catch one and slip him under the ice the way the other town did, they say. At least there is no more fighting. Even with half the crop turned into rotgut, according to the farmer who admits to selling it to some half-uniformed men, the Jayhawkers don't get up the courage to return, to ride into town shooting it up as if they have orders. Besides, the town put up such a good fight, nothing pretend about that at all. Why, for six weeks after, a green light burned all through the night in the last house, a signal to those of that sort not to bother with the town—a signal the town won and could repeat that win upon provocation.

Weighted with their own sorrows, they don't wonder that a young girl with a lame leg would run into the store and take it over without a claim. I am tall for my age and the baby confuses them too, he is so soon portly, looking in his plaid how any shopkeeper should in miniature. But it is really my lameness that convinces them. Lameness looks sincere—who walks with a limp if they don't have to? What lame girl would claim such booty with a babe-in-arms if she isn't rightful?

The cutting of cloth is not so different from moving sand or trapping. All that is wanted is the desire to cut. And the townspeople need black cut in abundance. The scissors and the ruler are all the tools I need—and a serious study of the ledger by way of prices, something I know about from figuring furs for Pa. But there comes a time that someone wants a shirtsleeve sewn just like the one that has suffered ruin, and he has no woman to do it for him, and as my uncle's niece, I should harbor such skills and must try.

Of needles and spools I'm not entirely ignorant. My sisters sewed and I do remember threading a seam together once or twice. The man agrees on a price and bargains for a needle and a length of thread to be thrown in, in case of rips. Scoffing, I let him show me how he would use them, being a man, and I watch him close. After he leaves me the shirt in its distress, I cut out a copy of the wanted sleeve, though I cut it too narrow without allowing for the seam, and have to cut it again. Then I get so powerfully intent on sewing it right that I sew the seam to my own skirt. I have to light another lamp and sew it all over again, puckering the extra material at the last, under the arm.

He only complains when he throws his arm out that the cloth is congested.

The baby really likes you, I say instead of *Sorry*. Give the baby a kiss.

How do I know that he is a man so womanless that he harbors a disgust for babies he never can get over? My own Pa could guess about a person just from seeing his hat.

Here is your money, the man says, and he puts his arm down quick.

Soon every wagon coming or going has a Bust this or that on its side, and each one is carrying hope on the tails of violence, Mr. Lincoln's war or the Indian's. A wagon rolls in with a story of ladies burnt up when their dresses blew into a campfire so I sell shot to sew into the hem for cooking on windy days. Don't drown on the river crossings, I warn them, these hems are heavy. All their wagons make the town busy most of the time and me too, or else I'm standing at the counter, watching for Pa or the girls or Sharon. The baby sprouts a red color hair with his portliness but I tell myself it's the color of contentment, not of anybody's who hasn't come back. As soon as I get extra money, I put an ad for Pa in the territory newspaper that people pass from hand to hand and that I have read and pined over, remembering how to read. The headline picture shows Lincoln's son in his coffin, a boy of eleven, and I wipe my eyes after, boys being what I find feeling for, and there's another picture with skaters stiff against the cold of the city of Washington, muffed and gliding along the river there. The baby brings me back soon enough, or customers, and I fold that newspaper with its headlines and ad and go back to work. After a while, the few trappers who do stop by tell me it's all trapped out where I am, not to bother with a lookout.

I keep all the trapping supplies fresh anyway, trading for what the wagon trains bring. But I don't follow them, not even the go-backs. If I stay in one place I figure anybody can find me. One place shows all the prints, as all trappers and Pa well knows. You have to wander when you have nothing. Pa did not have the luck I have, to stay. Here is something, I say to the baby. Even if everybody is on half-credit, it is still a real something with no heir to the shopkeeper hurrying into town to claim it. But there comes a time when folding the growing boy into his sheets I hear the baker's wife go through my accounts.

After her report, four men come in an elect offering to help me in my business. I am ready. I produce a letter that greets me as "a shopkeeper's true happiness," and hearkens to our labors together as kin. Nevermind that the hand is similar to mine—most of the men need spectacles to read anyway and don't have them and can't afford to buy those I could sell them. They just nod over the paper while I hold it for them to read. The others mouth the paper's words slowly and make their own nods while I remind each and all of them how I have bound their dead, I have clothed their wives, I have treated their babies with sugar by the handful. I tell them to help themselves to the crackers. I remind the oldest of his debt to me of the wagontop pants I've mended myself out of my own thread. They are threadbare now, I tell him in front of the others, why not stop embarrassing yourself and buy a new pair?

The boy drags out a length of cloth as if on cue, and says nothing, the way he always does, to the applause and laughter.

Two

Chapter 13

Blossom, leaf fall, snow—the peddler arrives at the turn of the first year and climbs onto the new boardwalk in a slick silk frockcoat and a hat as high as bird's nest balanced on his ears. Oy! you! he says, opening my door. He rubs his back as if the time I pulled him down with his wares is today, as if I hadn't watched him wielding his tricks with the Indian who wanted some bottle he could not get, or quarreled with him the day he figured the actual true date of my release, as if surprise has hit him.

You must've found a nugget on Indian land, I say and point past him at his wagon with what is surely a stolen horse it is so good pawing the snow melting in front of it.

Don't stand in the sun if you have butter on your head, he laughs. I heard the shopkeeper was felled, he says, and that his niece and a boy took his place—but you? And a boy?

I cross my arms. The uncle wrote for us.

The peddler removes his hat, looks at it, sticks it back on his head. Madam, he says, with a little bow.

I curtsy fast.

Just as fast, he's squinting at my stock. You're charging too much for the worsted. I'll charge less, he says.

I'm sure you can. You want to run me out of business?

Retail, schmetail. I'd rather you talk to customers, he says. He flips back the end of his silk coat and settles on a stool. You can curry the customers to buy what I bring, and I can bring such loads as big as you order—his arms spread to show how much—easy to transport with a wagon as commodious as the one now in my equipage. And with one more big order like the one you will give me, I won't have to travel clear to the coast to work with Levi, that troublesome cousin of mine who is feeding and clothing all those ignorant miners. Credit, that's all you need, he says to me like it's settled.

I tell him I am glad to see him.

He bends to his bag and comes up with a card of pins, his name printed across the card, which he offers. You are as straight as a pin, he says, which is good for credit, and besides, I know you by your Indian hardship. I can refute anyone who says you limp out of self-misery.

Self-misery? I say. I examine the pins for rust. Any child who has fallen from her uncle's carriage at such a speed should be grateful to walk at all.

He stops unfolding a length of silk tucked deeper in his bag. Oh, such a terrible fall. He winks.

I can't keep from whispering, What about Pa? You've been across the country again and back.

He folds and unfolds his wares, tightens a patent medicine top. He puts his hand over mine. He says, No Pa with daughters looking as nice as you.

Oh! My hand moves quick to be with my other.

He rushes on to say, I have to beg a favor of you—and he lofts his hand as if it had never fallen so close to mine.

Yes?

Madam, he says with new gravity. I had already come to an agreement with the dead shopkeeper and I wish to affirm it with you. I have heard—he leans close—I know about the size of your cellar.

There is nothing to the size of my cellar, I say. Two of your pins and three jars of preserves could fit inside it. Only took-apart wagon boards keep it from caving in.

Your cellar abuts the bluff, he says.

No, I say. There's a distance you have to walk before the bluff.

There's a rock at the bluff and a way into the secret side of your cellar. The shopkeeper showed me.

You know a lot about my cellar I don't. What would a shopkeeper want such a big cellar for anyway? I say. There's bare shelves here as it is.

He had another business of which I was privy to, says the peddler, brushing the silk of his hat with that hand of his.

I don't think I want to know about it, I say.

I have some lovely lace you could have, he says. Not the tatting I sell to the Indians.

As close to lace I know are the rag bandages I've been rolling for the St. Louis Sanity Fair. I catch the tail of the twisted linen thread he's dangling from his watch pocket. A lot of holes in it.

There are slaves—he whispers, and stops.

There's no end to the blood of boys shed over slaves these days, I say.

He unrolls the better paper-wrapped lace. The shopkeeper hated and detested the business of slavery, he goes on, and I now aid and abet the conveyance of those who escape. Soon enough the war and its doings will be over, but until then—

You do have a secret.

He holds up a nice V of lace, lace for a neck. This lace bewitchment here mimics God's humble creature, the spider in her nest. All things are caught in lace. I want to use your cellar for my business, he says, laying the lace on the back of his hand, let me pay your freight too. Free freight, he says, for the shepherd who believes in helping out with a flock.

I was a slave, I say. I wouldn't want to pay to escape.

You had a term and served it, he says. The children go free.

I make my way to the back of the store, limping still on account of my slavery. Hiding slaves that flee is a riddled proposition. They were bought people, I say. I am a shopkeeper now.

No one will imagine it of you, he says, following me. You, with your boy cousin, claiming the best business in town. His smile opens over his teeth. Is he your cousin really?

My eyes stretch open wide.

So, by lending me this cellar—he heads back to his wares—you will be doing good, helping slaves to freedom. Where else will they go?

Well—they have my sympathy is what you can count on, I say.

The bell over the door rings.

Surely this gingham will fade, I say loudly. Don't you have a surer pattern that the women here will not soon grow tired of?

Perhaps this sample. The peddler shoots his hand into his bag.

Two ladies crinoline their way up to my counter where the peddler tips his hat, one hand still rustling in his bag.

There's a lot of competition in silk shirtwaists these days, he says, what with the new illustrateds. He produces a magazine instead of the sample. Would you two like to purchase a subscription? I deliver twice yearly in time for the swing of fashion.

How dear would it be? asks the lady eyeing instead the lace neck that still drapes the counter.

Ten cents a copy.

The other customer says she never has time to read the papers anymore, not even an illustrated, that the telegraphs soon to come pouring in will make even more reading she has to find time for. But they don't hesitate to paw through the peddler's wares as soon as they're spread over the counter. Give the orders to her, he says after he enumerates their cost, item by item.

Top rail! they exclaim as they go off and out my door, convinced of happiness but I'm sure suffering trepidation having parted with actual cash, the way shoppers always feel.

See how fast it sells, the peddler boasts.

I have to smile.

He belts his last box shut after I take samples and write my order. He tucks it back into his bag quick but uses the time to tell me the Indian's mound curls just like a snake now that it is built.

You must know what is going on everywhere, I say.

He lifts the bag in one hand, it is that light now, he tilts his head. Are you calling me a spy?

I don't back off. I say, the Indians, in particular, need spies. The way they now find themselves kept and bought off or killed, worse than those slaves you have me taking.

Mensch, he says. I am slave to you.

It is not six days later while the boy and I are hunting rabbit tracks in the snow that I spot a shadow cross toward the bluff. The boy is pretending to jump like a rabbit to lure it so he doesn't notice. That night I tell him my Pa taught me that bread in a cellar feeds dreams all night and since the cellar has no stairs—it's just a hole in the floor with wide, unsquared planks, parts of a chest from Bohemia or Norway or St. Petersburg wedged upright against one wall—I use a rope to lower a loaf down, wrapped in a bolt end I can't sell it's so faded. One for the soul, I say, one for the body which we eat, and I leave our third loaf locked up to sell. The boy says the mice will certainly have good dreams, but says nothing more about it as a loaf a day is about right for us. I keep on leaving loaves in the cellar though I hear nothing from the other side of its door, nor see sign of anyone of any color at the bluff again. Not that I want to. I have my own dreams about slave life and they are not good. I could go down and give whomever the benefit of my bondage, but no one can take me back, claiming my skin destinates me for slavery forever. Those in my cellar are wise to the way of escape, being always in the state of desperation, and could find my advances and claims loathsome. If anyone asks, I am filling my cellar with bread for a famine, and as for the bluff, I have seen only the shadows, with nothing bodily behind them. I heard an Omaha man say about the free ones they get there, that their color shines against the night, looking like an Indian with grease on him.

One snowy morning I find the bread still tied to my rope.

Do my neighbors guess? They have so much to do with farming and building they can scarcely keep track of the comings and goings of their own kin, let alone visitors. Besides, I have to hold the lie of my survival too close to be friendly, I am too honest to do otherwise. Oh, I dance when they do, to whatever is fiddled, though never a waltz, not since that dream, and I laugh when they say I'm lame and shouldn't be dancing. If they knew how I danced those years for the Indian! At the beginning they were short of women, the hard life that it was, and men danced with scarves tied to their arms to show they took the woman's part. I always had to dance then and played cool to the men with scarves and those without—I knew slavery when I saw it.

All the cowboys with their herds moving through serve up more distraction. They sing from their hymnbooks while camped at the edge of town amidst their lowing doggies, then without their books they sing in town in the saloons. The town endures the stink of these saloons for the cowboys' cash. After they finish all their singing, they play cards and drink so much they vomit on the floor, and then they drink more. Quite a lot of them overstay and miss their herds and end up having to do the spring calving. Instead of the judge hearing the worst of their roughhouse cases outside in the wide open where anybody can object and find rope and a friend to haul the poor souls up some tree, preachers arrive with tents to have one and all swear sobriety, but then those same cowboys gamble in those same tents in the months after the preachers leave, until an actual courthouse is considered.

Where, no one can agree on.

Soon enough a wagon stops, heaped with the new canned goods, and its owner sets up shop across town with all the *How do you do* in the world. So many wagon trains coming by, loaded with people sick of war but wanting promise and provisions even more than peace—I don't begrudge him. I change to keeping mostly dry goods and doing more of the sewing. People envy a seamstress less. It appears as if she is doing actual work rather than just trading for profit.

So nobody's watching me close, what with the new shop and a war still raging, blue against grey, a regular bruise, and the Indians being hunted by what few troops are left, and these cowboys who are starting to annoy the settlers with ideas about their rights regarding fences and other such impediments to making the money that they in turn want to spend in the settlers' town's bars.

Or else everyone's watching everything like they do in any town.

Chapter 14

William the Hat says, Leave the mound. He says it's time to take the ponies to the far pasture and get out of the way of the wagons.

The land is not theirs or ours, says the Indian. He is smearing green paint over his cheekbones. He will paint red dots over them, and a slash of white across his forehead where his worries show. Or else red there too.

The army has collected all the children just a day's ride away. What does that mean? William the Hat does not raise his voice, does not insist on meaning. He is a believer in logic. Taking children away to a school when they have crops to cut, crops they made us plant is not logical, Indian or otherwise.

They need braves to fight for their black people, even children will do with all the men they have killed. They are so busy with all that killing and collecting money from people to pay for their war that they don't think about crops, about us eating. They think buffalo fall at our feet. Remember when they flew a ball into the sky out of blood that they then burnt while they were riding inside it?

William turns up his hat brim his own paint has stained

in a blue blot. A balloon. They are crazy and they make us crazy.

The Indian smiles, and some of his white paint flakes off his cheek. What about another color?

You can still back off, says William. Take the ponies so your other brothers will have them for trade later. I don't know about more color.

The Indian nods like he is considering his good counsel but really he is just trying to feel where his hair parts, where he should put another line. I will stay here beside my mound, he says.

His headdress flutters: dragonflies and butterflies across the brow, a forked-tail swallow he has sewn himself between the two rows of eagle feathers down his back. He looks good when he has to.

If you stay, the women have to stay. William squares his hat on his head. Horse Fat and the others will give you big trouble about that. They are saying the snake is alive now.

Finally, says the Indian.

UNREST! UNREST! INDIANS SLAUGHTER SETTLERS

Land's sakes alive, I say. The ragged old Homestead Act paper is pinned up right beside the headline. Can't people put two and two together?

Some slaves going for homesteads too, says the Norwegian with an accent thicker than any slave or Indian. Maybe the Indians going homesteading too. He smiles inside his dirty white homesteading beard and pats the boy who jigs my hand with boy impatience.

I shake my head the way I shook hands with the Norwegian—warily. The horse we are hoping to fight over is tied to the old pony express hitching post. To make the speed of those horses rub off on this old hayburner? The Norwegian and myself, with such words as can be understood between us, exchange this thought, slow-stepping away from such notices the old express office likes to post, and toward the sale horse.

The horse suspects us. If he could talk he would ask what we intend with our prodding and teeth-checking, having never been sold before, or so the owner, a bit short on teeth himself, swears.

The owner is slight and fervent.

In such unrest, you need a top horse, says the owner. He can't keep from smiling while we look at the horse's gums, and showing off his own. The horse has the hair of the boy who is now bent to the ground using his set of marbles—that red. The owner says the color of his horse indicates a good speed, he says the soldiers out to protect the telegraph need this horse, would pay top dollar, but they are on far patrol.

I am in the market for a horse. I don't mind a six-mile walk to fit someone for their final resting clothes or riding the wagon the rich rich McKaffners send to change all their waists, but I feel a real need now, with the boy old enough to ride with me—why, I should lift my head out of the seams and get around myself. I can, at last, afford it. I don't worry so much about Indians, wild or otherwise.

The Norwegian produces a carrot out of his pants pocket that will take the guesswork out of the horse's bite and overall vim, he says. He places and moves his hands on its warm neck while the animal eats. Unrest with the Indians is how we get the land here, he says.

I hear there's a peck of bandits out there too, who used to

work for the pony express, says the owner, men making off with stolen money and stock. You need a horse to protect yourself.

The horse swallows.

This is not a known horse, all the known horses are hired or harnessed. I ask how the horse truly was come by. The owner sucks his teeth, he says it is his own horse that he rode all the way in from his homestead some forty miles yonder, and he is on foot after this, he has to walk to a train and with this money pay a fare to ride at least as far as Chicago where another train leaves. This is his third homestead, he says, and he has nothing left but his horse out of his whole time here. He spreads his hands to include the here of all our sparse everything, mostly the three real houses that have gone up since I stumbled in, and the ten or so more soddies, the courthouse and the express office. He chews on a cigar that seems like something extra he would be hard put to afford.

The Norwegian is nodding and nodding, though both the owner and myself believe that all he understands is the word Chicago, where he left his own train and picked up the grit that the owner seems to have lost.

I am dragging this out, this money spending. The boy is petting the nose of the horse but it looks as if it will nip, it is that tired-looking. How much will you take from me? I ask.

The Norwegian will give more.

I step away from the beast and its look of suspicion, I step around it. The bones of its haunch are what the Indian called flying, the kind that makes the eater, if he would eat horseflesh, wish his jaws could fly.

I say more again but when the Norwegian touches the thin red flank and pulls up a hoof, I back down from another bid,

I say, More horses coming no matter whose side wins, grey or blue or brown.

I must appear wistful watching the Norwegian prod the horse down the street with a switch because the ex-owner says, I wasn't about to sell it to you, a woman all alone with a boy in a place like this. You just helped the price.

Chapter 15

The thunderstorm won't stay put. Lightning runs sideways, cloud-to-cloud, thunder crackles with echo, a double rainbow shimmers before the rain even starts, but no tornado hangs from a yellow cloud—yet. The boy and I keep inside, all our windows tight, the candelabra lit in the dark, the door gap jammed with a doubled length of rope in case of flood.

So far the storm is just loud and dry.

Let's pretend you are my mother, says the boy.

I drop two stitches and pull my wool ball closer. Thunderstorms loosen his tongue. I am your cousin, I say.

The boy is laying chess pieces on their sides, he is watching me from his crinkled pale eyes. Boys six have a way of getting old when they want to. Let's have my mother alive instead, he says. Let's pretend. I've heard other boys pretend. It was a day like this, he says.

I put down my tatting and thrust the shovel head into the flames, its handle burnt one coal-fired day and now the metal end of it lies around in amongst the arrowheads and chess pieces he plays with, I thrust that shovel head into the fire and stir it. It was like night, on a morning like this, I say. Seeing the sudden severity of the boy's set face sense what I'm saying is truth, I go on. It wasn't all the same exactly. You lived in a lean-to in Mt. Airy, a town that isn't there anymore. I don't think I could find even the tracks.

If my real Ma were to come in right now, he says, I'd think up words for her. To have stood out in lightning!

I say nothing. What words I'd have with Pa and my sisters—a real storm.

The boy says nothing more. There would be pleasure in sharing the mottled-over past but where would I stop with the sorrow? Only this last year has he begun playing with other boys, boys with dirty collars and pockets heavy with rocks, found insects, and wadded string, boys who cry for their mothers and laugh when they come, and I am happy for him.

The shovelhead glows at the tip where it touches the flame too long. I pull it out. It glows the red of his hair, he is sitting there red-lashed and -headed like no Bulgarian he's supposed to be.

We know what we know, I say. Your mother and father are dead. Dead from the touch of lightning.

They are your relations too.

Shshshsh, I say. It is so sad. I pick up my tatting again and tat faster.

What about other brothers? he asks. Other families have more to them.

There was another sister, I say.

You never told me about her.

I told you. She died too, she held your mother's hand.

Anyone else?

No, no one.

And Uncle sent for us both?

I nod.

I own the lightning, he says, with fierceness deep in his unused voice. Like a god of lightning from the far county, the one the Swedes are always on about.

Thor, I say. The one god my Pa liked but I don't say so. I might lose him if I talked about Pa and he told, the two of us being unrelated and living together like this, even with me raising him.

He takes a few steps away from the fire, he lifts the chess piece. I throw my lightning down, he says. I am angry with this mother whose husband plows my land in the lightning time.

And a sister, I say just as he hurls the chess piece to the floor.

Pick that up, I say. One of the ears is already broken.

While he is planted all fours to the floor, fetching it from under the furniture, the cellar creaks.

The boy stiffens.

Must be a ghost, I say.

Customers like ghosts, he says.

This is something I said. Sometimes they don't, I say and roll my tatting to get up and walk around, to make the floor noisier.

He collects the horse, he goes to stand at the window.

It's too stormy to be so close to the window but I don't say that. I say, disturbed by so much talk from him and the creaking hinge, What should we pretend now?

The boy just taps the horse to the window.

I press my hand over his to keep the window from breaking. Orphaned, but not forgotten like me, he has only me to forgive. He doesn't look up or even move so we are both staring through the glass when the tornado cloud dips.

We run and climb into the cellar, we crouch beside the jars

I squeezed in not a week earlier, the tomatoes being fruitful and everyone liking our spiced conserves. I prefer to put them in the shop window where the light cuts through the stringy bits, making the fruit hard to resist, but we had too many. It is so dark here you can hardly see the jars with your nose right to them.

He has never been down here before. He is a curious boy like any other but the hole I showed him is so dark and small it doesn't hold his interest. I think.

Stop shaking, he says to me.

The promised land! We swap places, hind to heart—and I feel the shaking too, the slave pressed tight against the door in fear.

It's nothing, I tell him.

The boy laughs. I know nothing, he says.

Maybe I do shake, now and then, I say.

This time the house shakes—from a strong gust, and there are crashes, big ones. My glass pane? I crimp my knees, trying to make myself smaller and so does the boy. We bend down, flatten out our talk. I hear *Pray!* from the boy.

Another crash.

This is the occasion, he says.

I think up words, for him but not for me who wants bees to hum only in the fields, porridge with chew, and payment upon presentation. A kind of prayer too, when you think about it. I pray loud.

Rain begins in the middle of our "Glory be's," rain like a big relief, and a trickle starts from a crack in a floorboard it comes down so hard so fast. Then there's a groaning, what they call a spiritual by those who sing them, "King Jesus A'listening," then "The Old Sheep Know the Road," and

"Ain't Gonna Tarry Here." It sounds as if the whole house is torn apart while there is this singing, and the boy looks at me.

I act like I don't hear. Even after we get ourselves up and climb out of the hole as slow as if the world down there is the sweetest place and we had come to hear about it, I say nothing, and he keeps that wise look of his.

Chapter 16

Slow water flows its single file across my front, down my cleft with its new dark growth so like the chokecherry bushes riverside that hang over me. I've pegged clean clothes on a line from a bush to the bluff overhead with my naked self lying under a regular criss-cross tent-town of fresh laundry, one white cotton house after another, all of them helping to shield my soaking self from any neighbor's eye.

Soaking is so refreshing, after all the labor.

Townspeople tend to wash at the pump anyway. I myself should not like to wash at the river after all my sand hauling but a lightness comes over me taking the path to it because it isn't sand I'm hauling, only my own and other people's laundry for extra money on a Saturday. I wash it all clean and then I bathe in the slow water after, while the clothes dry on the bushes and on my pegs. No one complains about the color of his shirtfront after I scrub it.

I should be washing the boy too, arm and crotch, but he hurt himself on a loose barrel stave running after chicks and he did cry. It wears them out to cry. But he isn't supposed to chase critters, wild or not, through the store. The stave took care of my heeding. He is sleeping with a bandaged toe.

In Bohemian, there is a word for the air quivering over ripening cherry trees at noon. On my tongue tip. How I long for those trees or even an apple or a plum. I stop sanding my ankle with river bottom mud and hold still, sure the Bohemian words will arrive.

Miz Emma, I hear called from the direction of where the third shirt is strung, Miz Emma.

Then I hear a horse canter and two people—

They got their sheets and all out, says the man's voice.

Like as not, says the girl. Let's steal them.

Let me steal a kiss instead, says the man.

Not here.

There is this little covey I know. I'll scare out the jackrabbits and such and make a place. Come on.

I hear a fuss not too far away and lie as flat as I can to the water.

I'll just sit, says the girl.

You just sit and take all my kisses or else. You are fifteen and must get one for every year.

It is not really my birthday today.

No matter, we will start on the next year soon anyway.

Be careful of my dress. The girl patched it.

Then it is not so strong there. Oh, you are as sweet as sin. One more kiss?

Wait—I think someone is coming.

—they scrabble up.

No, not a darn soul, says the man, sinking.

I'm sure someone's coming, maybe the girl for the wash is coming. Put your head up again and see what there is to see.

—a rustling silence.

You are a-thinking things, he says.

Someone's slapping at midges, I hear it.

They are not.

I hear it. Or else a sneeze.

A ghost?

—the two of them are standing again, the girl in a hurry.

Let's go on the horse a ways, she says.

Not yet, he says. I like your neck.

I'll catch the pony, she says. From the top of the pony, I can see practically into your brother's corn crop.

Hold up there, I'll get him. He might give you a nip.

—I can see the horse hooves they are that close.

I'll sit behind. Safer there from your "steering" hands.

I'll steer you yet, Missy. Look here, not a soul in sight. Let's get down again and celebrate your birthday right, what you say? I might be going off again to fight any day now.

The only war you got to go to is the one with me. Come on, Ma is going to start to wonder. Giddyup.

Missy! Darn you.

As soon as the galloping-off is over, I wet-arm myself into my apron dress, laughing. One of the prissiest girls I know, that Missy, yet always ready to show an ankle, and him—why, who would think of her on a horse with him?

I am still laughing and folding the laundry off the pegs when a lone man rides up.

He walks over to the water as if he is needing a year off a horse. IW or AWOL? In the war or out on his own hook?

Men have been showing up in town for months, bruised and broken and played out, sometimes three or four at a time, half dead. There is no parade to celebrate their return. They are not deserters, they say, the war is over enough or it ought to be and it's time to plant. Sometimes a man comes in off the street into my store and he is so thin he looks like his sister, yes, except for those wooden eyes. If he's missing a limb I discount the material accordingly. Or Old Man Rains arrives to buy six lengths on tick, and gives me a gun to keep because his son has gotten so used to shooting. He tells me to keep it shiny for later when the wrong side shows again—or in case his corn doesn't come in and the varmints do or the six buffalo left in the world stampede out of nowhere.

No one speaks much of a wrong side anymore, they talk around the subject, talk as if they're surprised to be speaking anywhere near it. The war time is behind us, thank god, God being just a figure of speech they use here with the war talk, when they are not talking Him up, taking up plowing time and sewing by thanking Him instead of the generals and all the dead boys.

God left with the balloon the devil dragged off, that's what I think. He hasn't been watching for storms or wars.

That this soldier's not lame in his walking surprises me. They're almost all lame, one way or another, just like me.

Jesus, the man swears, coming up from dunking his face in the river.

The bugs are worse over there, I tell him.

Henry, he says his name is after I ask. He rubs his face dry with his shirttail.

Spit in the sand for luck, I tell him, and I take in the last of the laundry.

Chapter 17

Sixteen is still a child, I say, and I am not a child drinker. Help yourself.

The peddler is rooting through a board box for a clear glass to pour my wine into, the bottle being payment for a button-up suit I made for a returned soldier with troubles who died drinking too much of it. I do love the smell though, I say, even with temperance talking up its evil.

Sometimes I sell it myself for the purposes of medicine, admits the peddler, pouring out a glass so he can sample it. Rumtopf is the other, he says. The Germans steep their rum with sugar. They say enough of it is sent across the mountains to keep every man in the territory of Montana inebriated all winter.

His speech is soon loosed into a steady slow flow, the way the river runs in dead summer until the fish can be speared out of it like carrots in a stew. He spears at the stew I find to set out for him to go with the plum wine, he drinks most of the bottle's worth.

I empty its last dark splash into his glass, and he tips it away from his tintype-bold so-pink lips, another new bit of him, pinked up this winter on account of a bad frost. May the seraphim-in-a-carriage arrive so scented, he winks, and then he insists I swallow this last as my own, which I do, just to taste the lovely smell.

Worse than your patent medicines, I cough.

He laughs like he's older. Here are more of your straight pins, straighter than a line laid down against the globe, he says with a flourish, producing them from out of his front pocket. But he keeps hold of them in his hand, teasing.

Yes, I say. My cellar still has visitors, despite the proclamation of freedom.

Such a proclamation is hard on the business, he says.

But their term is up.

It is difficult to tell from my end how much of the travel is due to lax implementation of the proclamation, or the timely movement of the people elsewhere in the habit of fear, or anger with those growers newly without labor leading to oppression. Leaning toward me, he releases the pins into my hands one at a time.

I feed them all nonetheless.

Something else is coming, he says. His voice goes deep with drink and drama as he announces: An opera.

He is so serious I laugh. He scuttles into himself, he thinks I mock, he shrugs and folds the empty pin paper into fours.

An opera with a famous voice? I say to carry him along. No one will come here to sing. Maybe a minstrel show.

They will sing, he says, pinching closed his bag. And not tra-la-la either. I have heard of them in the capital cities and this troupe is exceptional.

He stands and makes an uncertain turn of head not quite toward me, and then he walks through the store knocking at things—barrel, barrel, box—with the big bag that weighs his arm. A bit too much of the glass perhaps, he says, righting the crackers.

I hold open the door. You will need these for the opera tickets, he says. He fishes out two folded bills from in amongst his pocket items. The boy will like it.

The boy hardly speaks, let alone sings. An opera for him would be birds in springtime. He doesn't know music. I look at the bills in his outstretched hand.

Buy the tickets, he says. Or I will sing the lyrics for you. He tucks the bills in my hand, puts his hat on his head, singing three lines of something odd and loud.

That will frighten the boy for sure, I laugh.

I am a true tenor, he says. Next year I am going to quit selling and sing arias for all your customers and put you out of business.

You are welcome to try, I say. With so many girls looking for wedding silk every time a regiment is released, I am sewing my eyes to the cloth. I slave.

He grins at the secret word spoken between us.

I watch beside the door while he piles his wagon with bag on bag, its fenders shredded to tatters, the new old horse in front clearly a much poorer theft than the horse from before. The rush west that made him rich has slowed.

The wind, he says once he's seated, Hear it sing? Like an opera between backboards. But instead of taking off his hat and waving it when his horse jerks the load into motion, he hunkers down.

The wind does whip.

The opera is attended by townspeople in a flung-together opera house. They all peacock about, wearing mostly my clothes. I sew straight on until curtain time, I am plucking at a customer's loose thread in the foyer. But I am no fairytale cinder seamstress, I myself wear a green silk shirtwaist, bustled and tufted and with a little of the peddler's lace at the throat, the tiny bit he insisted on giving me, to advertise his business, he said. Even those just returned from the war brush their uniforms clean, their mothers and fathers or wives leading them along by the crooks of their arms as if the soldiers have forgotten how to walk, even Henry, the man I met at my washing whose mother has already hounded me for an extra button. The clothes of those who didn't return I have cut down for the children. The boy himself wears a cutdown jacket from a customer who went off from his wounds before he could pay me, and the boy doesn't despise it. He struts about on seven-year-old legs the jacket half covers, his red curls hidden under a hat that is soon found thrown in a snowdrift.

A dark-haired girl skirts him. She has just taken up residence in town, having come from a farm some one hundred miles west. She ignores as many of the town boys and girls as she can, given the difficulties of no one else worthy of her association. She is going to be a writer and she tells anyone who asks she is really from Virginia, though it seems they don't ask often enough, she is so anxious to put them right. When they do ask, she tells them her family has lived in Virginia for centuries, making her last word very long on the tongue. Are you from here? she asks my boy, who is swanning around in his cutdown jacket.

I come from lightning, he says. I was hurled down from the sky.

She exits for her seat with a flounce of her readymade dress. O, pioneers! she says half out loud in quick disdain, passing me.

Chapter 18

Sharon? I call out, limping into the barn.

The actress becomes herself with just a swipe of cold cream on a towel, enough paint gone to show her lost face fresh in the mirror she's hung on the siding. Sharonette on the notice, she says. You loved my part?

I didn't know it was you for sure until you stood on the boards in tableaux during the singing, I say.

Oh, she says. This town—I forgot it was here. She unwinds a bright new ribbon from around her dark wig. We have not done this region before. Because of the Indians. She squints at me. It is good to see you.

We don't clasp each other, though she does fling down the ribbon and hold out her hands. Would you like me to sign your playbill? she asks.

Was that the balloon silk waving for the fire? I say instead of answering.

It was, or some such old rag. She laughs and repeats her look of tableaux fear for me.

The prince acted the devil with the greatest of ease, I say.

The lieutenant can't get the curtain down fast enough after

I'm caught—they all want the prince to die too. With long sweeps of her hands, she unpins the wig.

But you are the princess now, I say.

I am the show princess. Sharon shakes out her own hair, as red as ever, then finds a brush lying on a traveler's chest and takes it to the wig. Sometimes I draw the customers by scattering the royal bills from the balloon, she says. You must have seen them. She scatters a few wisps of black wig-hair from her brush in a wide arc.

I wonder about her wayward gesture—is this drama or drink or something else? If she is not herself, the question *Why did you leave us?* isn't something I really want answered. Besides, if they stole her, she did well enough by the theft.

I say, You are not an inch taller.

Yes, she says.

I lean into the balls of my feet and back.

Sharon exchanges her skirt for a stained apron tied over her petticoats and begins to gather the hay from around the barn for her bed. I am treated well enough, she says.

Through the barn walls, well past the opera house steps, the prince bellows about a lost crown. Where is that crown?

The great long flame of her hair trails her back while she makes up her bed, sweeping the hay into a mound, throwing a blanket over it.

I don't move off.

Where is the baby? she says at last.

Boy, I correct her. They are not in the infant state forever. I sent him home. He has to rise early to do his chores before he goes to school. He enjoyed all the singing.

Is he tall?

He is not. He is like you—his real mother.

No, she says. You saw her dead. But her voice rises with this denial, rises like the hair released from her brush, floating in the cool air between us.

Here it is, shouts the prince, closer to the barn this time. It is all bent and ruined, you *Dumkopf*.

A bottle breaks.

Did you never find your Pa? Sharon faces me, her hands red where they grip each other.

I say No.

Maybe it is that name you took.

Surprised by her tack, I say, Pa is a hunter and a trapper. He could find me, name or no name.

Well. Sharon inspects me.

I put an ad in a paper but the only two replies wanted to know if I would take them in and care for them even if they didn't turn out to be Pa.

The prince pulls back the barn door and enters with scenery folded end-to-end. The tree! he says, with the fervor of effort. He nods, seeing me—just a bend of his neck without a crick of *Hello*—and says to her, Paint it over.

Black? she says.

It is winter all through the scene! he says with the same impatience and accent as before. White of course, he says, and he throws up his hands and makes his exit, but not before he leaves a blue bottle with the paint can.

She snatches at the bottle as if it will fly away on its own.

I'm not surprised that the prince doesn't know me, I'm so differently dressed and older. Not that I want him to. What do you say to the devil? I watch Sharon take a quick drop from the bottle then hide it, with shaking hands, inside the chest.

Is there anything to do about the boy? she says, still at the chest, turned from me.

I am touching her hung-up satin skirt, its gold sash hanging from a peg, and the wig especially. It is not a question of doing now, I say. I have done what was needed.

Sharon opens the can of paint, daubing white here and there over the black below the tree and its branches. If you step back and hold it this way, she says, the tree is a rabbit.

I lift the wig from its place. If you step back, I repeat, and unfold the wig onto my head.

She turns from her painting and laughs. You are me, utterly.

I am glad to see you alive, I say.

She tells me she traveled all the way to the apple-bearing valleys where the grass stays green even with snow on the ground, and that she has a stick from there, *sans blossoms*, that she says that she would like me to have. She remembers how I played that the weeds at the fort were my orchard, and perhaps this stick will root. Then she wraps it in a rag wet from the jug it comes out of, its water thawed in the lamplight and the warmth of the two of us in the tight shut barn, and presents it.

I am not one to say if anything will happen for me in one of these apple valleys, she says. But a farmer with two bays and a fine homestead promises if I sing to him at apple bud time, he might marry me.

She sighs. All those beautiful apples.

Not oranges, I say.

She paints more white over the white. Why do you say oranges?

I just guess that a person like you might have wanted an

orange, really wanted one once, and that someone might have taken advantage of that.

She stops painting, a drip stripes her wrist.

No one will take advantage of you, she says.

The men here don't find me coquettish enough, I say, holding her gift at arm's length. And I limp. Oh, Sharon, I say, catching up her hand in my laden one. He is a dear boy.

All boys are dear, she says. You might send me a likeness of him I could carry with me. She lays down her paintbrush and rummages through the chest again and withdraws a sock containing the locket we found after the lightning struck her people, a gold heart that still opens to emptiness. I threw away the hair inside, she says. Soon I will have saved enough for a chain.

I thought to have a likeness done in a year or so when the boy looks more like his finished self, I say.

She laughs. You could find savings even in a boy's picture. Shutting the heart closed tight, she slides it back into the sock. Last year we had two helpers who swept the chimneys of all Philadelphia, young boys really, who sang inside the chimneys so they'd know which way to turn. They did the small parts well enough but died of the coal-cough before the tour was through. The boy—

—the boy won't come. I tap my stick gift to my hand with certainty. Where can I send you the likeness?

She looks into her mirror again, and moves a curl. Oh, send it wherever you hear the balloon will land. We travel to all the very best venues.

What I hear is that she will not be back. Our town is named Red Cloud, I tell her. You can't forget that.

Named it after seeing our balloon, did they? She laughs loud, the way she does onstage.

No, no—after the brave who went to the president about the Indian troubles—not that the town pulls for them.

Oh, very good, very good. She throws her hands up and claps to more of her own laughter. Red Cloud, she says again, in mirth. Immortalizing an Indian. Then she takes a few steps in her worn slippers across the swept floor, bends to open the chest again to return the locket, and finds a playbill she has signed. Tell the boy I'm famous, she says, with the bill outstretched in her hand.

I consider her in the leavings of her princess dress and her careful smile, the paint smeared fingers with the white coiling up her wrist, and all that red hair.

I never told him about you, I say. He doesn't know you exist.

She looks down at the playbill. She looks down.

Chapter 19

To celebrate the statehood, women lay dozens of pies, meat and fruit, on one end of all the tables in town pushed together, and lever kegs of drink onto the other end. The men are forced to bathe for the event, which they maintain is truly ridiculous. How is a bath political? Their wives and mothers trim their mustaches and beards and polish their buttons and find shoes for them that make them look as if they had marched into churches instead of battles. Many of the men take to giving and receiving kisses while all this is being done, some of the statehood beer having been leaked from the kegs. Thus the women are reminded of how much they missed them while they were warring, and how fearful they were falls out on their lips, or else they get short with them with all their feelings laid out like that.

I remember the drummer boy at the fort and turn a cracker tin into a drum that the shortest of the veterans takes, but I have to show him how to hold the sticks I have smoothed, I have to beat out a tat-a-tat for him. I only stole cattle, he tells me. I was good for that and as a prisoner. He doesn't have the soldier's disease, wanting only to smoke ground wild poppy, and he turns out to be one of the best eaters.

I am shocked by how many of the returnees do not match their relatives' descriptions. Some of it is in their size—described as barrel-chested, the man turns up deflated, unstaved. Do the women or the children or the old parent remember them wrong? The cheerful ones sing melancholy airs and the melancholy tell jokes. A rogue brother appears out of the prairie for the party, and he is so steadied out of his usual ways that his sister takes him in with not so much as a *toodle-do*. Even more shocking are the women and the children who stayed and starved whom the men don't recognize.

But all of the men congratulate themselves on themselves surviving, backslapping and cajoling, as if the survival is solely on their own account. Must be the strongest and cleverest, that family of six boys, all of them back, but one look and you see none of them could muster the courage to flush a woodpile for badgers. But not all of the returnees feign bravery. Some of the bravest could be wearing skirts, they fear even the sound of the ax, let alone the blast of the cannon that plenty shoot off for the statehood, the band playing in between volleys. Some of them can't figure out why they came back at all, and parade with their arms stiff at their sides and not around their wives. Others lift half-grown calves to show off what strength they returned with, a couple are loud about the women they fought off elsewhere, but all of them, brave or not, volunteered. That the statehood struggled to pass, having senators wanting to keep the vote to those of their own race until the President himself put in his objection, is nothing they want to discuss.

I am glad the slaves are free.

Before all the feasting, we play croquet in the wheat stubble, the cut rows making it harder on the cross shots but easier to hit the balls home. Every step rains grasshoppers. Afterwards, the horses throw off their shoes in the heat and two men compete throwing them at stakes beside the weighted tables, even heavier now that they're laden with slow-roasted haunches and the parts of chickens. All this food is remembered by count for decades, so many mock apple pies, so many legs of beef, and enough secret bottles and flasks besides the kegs under the table that no one knows how all the speeches—also counted—were ever finished. Men with sashes cut from cloth in colors so gaudy I couldn't sell them anyway stand and repeat themselves in the style of the day, ornately, with the vigor of new affirmation. Listeners beat their spoons at every *Grand Army of the Republic*, but louder when the dead president's name greets their ears as the choice for the new state capital's, two days' ride away.

Even Henry rises and tells about his serving the country as a cook. First he warms up the subject with *An Gorta Mor*, The Great Hunger that brought him and his mother over from their country shorn of their every relative, and how this spread of food here proves he emigrated for the good—he pokes his hand out toward the fly-laden empty rashers and scraped tin pots—and how half the shavetails he fought with weren't speakers of English at all but had struck the continent with about the same luck he had at about the same time, one war or another being what they were really good for, except for the eating. Old Tar, they called me, he says, on account of the supplies I used, and, of course, the taste of my cooking. Someone tells him to sit down, he is putting the fear of food into them, and for the first time I see a smile split his whiskers.

Chapter 20

While we are washing up, the ladies get to saying how well sewing bees renew the spirit and will stitch up the town tight and warm with concern and industry. They are all older than me but none of them run a business alongside childrearing and housekeeping. Wanting the company, I say I'm agreeable to a bee, but I also play up my industry. More needlework! It will never end. I tell them my preference: the sewing of whole clothes is like building a house but the straight-along quilt kind of sewing is the wagon train all over again. I stop short and don't mention I didn't come by train, I say those are very small stitches whichever way you put them in. We all laugh about that but quilting those straight lines together is the point of a bee, no getting around it.

I appear on the proper day, boy in tow.

He slinks to his knees with all the others his age, he crawls under the frame to dwell beneath its batting and cotton layers stretched waist-height for easy needle-picking. I envy him that twilight of hand shadows, there's the whisper and giggles of play, whereas above, the ladies, doing their one-two-three stitching with the sharpest of needles, gossip to beat the band. They say what nobody ought to know about themselves and others: two boys and what they did to the scrawny chicken, whose husband put an actual gold piece in the collection and took it back, in what way the cowboy's codpiece flaps open.

Maybe they invited me and the boy to take us down a peg. One woman says she sewed her first quilt at age eight, a 10 by 12. She still has it, carried it all the way here in a barrel from the East. Another woman's little girl doesn't join the under-the-quilt rascals but sits at her mother's knee, pushing a needle in one side and out the other for a Duck's Foot quilt, about as complicated a pattern you can sew. Even the woman with a hook-hand aims to out-quilt me, nose to the cloth, not taking a breath.

Then it comes: guessing that the boy has reached about eight years, they tell me that they have formed a committee to collect the funds to send the boy off to the new dumb school two states away. They have heard him talk, yes they have, but not often, not often enough.

I sew, I watch my fingers work.

In a whisper, I offer a double-handled milking pail to the woman beside me who heads that committee, the one who now insists he recite the Lord's Prayer for her out loud the day after harvest or else he must go, for his own sake, soon. I suspect she suspects his position on the Lord's Prayer is like mine. She won't take the pail, she doesn't have to, the money is already collected. They are just waiting for harvest to be over, when they can spare a horse to take him there. He has until then, time enough for other boys to learn the words even if they have never heard them before in their lives, words he must already know. He must pass that test after harvest, she says. Or else we will do our helping. And all that whistling of his, she says, doesn't count.

Fear escapes into the next row of stitches I make in the cloth. They curve.

The boy whistles opera, is whistling it now, under the quilt. No one knows how he remembers it, the opera having come and gone over a year ago. He whistles it more than he speaks these days, he whistles it beside the pump while the dishes get rinsed, standing as still as a horse or a cow in the dusk, with one hand raised in a pose. This frightens the townspeople, though they all saw it at the opera. Boys do not pose. Their offering to send him to school confirms their belief that he is just my ward, not my son, and that their good will is good. Or else they do it to test me, a far too biblical test for my taste.

Coffee is served at last, with everybody bringing out their cups, and someone divides a vinegar pie to share with something else got up—flour twigs rolled in sugar. I crumb my treat and listen to them talk on and on, waiting for a break to tender my resignation, as they call it in the town committee. It is all the straight seams, I say. I say I am happy enough to do a crazy quilt and even have pieces in my store I could bring, but I know they are not the fashion. The ladies are sad about that, maybe they could start a crazy quilt division that would meet the only other day I am closed, on Sunday afternoons, but one of them is more religious than the others and can't come, and then the others start to feeling that religious too.

I am gathering up my spools when the boy pulls down the far leg of the stretcher in a fight. Of course he won't say why or whatfor about it. He might have heard the committee's plan for him and balked on his own. It's not common that he finds a fight and the ladies know it, but I have to cuff the boy for the trouble.

I grip his arm after, and smile, and all the ladies smile back with their politeness.

Despite my beliefs, I have him repeat the prayer slow whenever he is still enough, and once before sleep, and first thing after rising while we haul water for the orchard. It galls me to do it, *Our father!* Of course the boy will know the prayer. I promise him a whole sausage for his performance before the committee lady, he who remembers nothing about a balloon and a prince or the balloon fire, just the savor of a spicy meat sucked through his gums. He lets me order a special sausage just for him from the peddler. You don't want to be in a place that will make you speak at will, I tell him, where they will work you in a workshop, day and night and not for yourself?

Behind his pale eyes—those eyes that should be mine by now if time and tenderness had any sway in looks—I hope he makes his plans.

Chapter 21

A dough that's sung to enough will lift its brick of flour and be light in the hand and on the stomach. Bohemians have a song for when it's put to rise. I sing it loud, laying loaves inside a greased box, their tops as smooth as a baby's bottom, putting them far enough from the embers for the heat to help them swell but not bake. Not yet.

Brushing the little flour left on my fingers across my apron, I smell, over the bread yeast, rancid fat rubbed with sage or the leaves of a red bush.

Indians.

They walk their single file on the trail between the river and the back of my store to where I'm cooking. Indians like to visit me. They know I don't fear them like the others and I know they don't talk about me—they talk to no one. They spy on the store until they see no one in it then slink in to buy fishhooks, to turn their noses up at the pickles I still keep. I let the people in town think I'm brave.

They walk through my stump-stick orchard so smoothly not a leaf stirs. Even good Indians you are supposed to fear now, though the difference between good and bad is hard for any settler to know, what with all the noise about their troublemaking and our retaliations. I still think that noise is more about homesteaders and the railroad coming through, *Get those Indians out of the way*. Whatever the reason, these Indians who approach are from the same tribe as the Indian I slaved for, I can see by the shape of their heads, their hide bags—the few that still have them—so I don't worry. I worry for them, I have seen so few Indians of late. And none of their kind.

They harbor such a fear of settlers they don't even try to talk to me, they just brush past me to rifle through my goods, though one of them does stand a foot away, dangling an arrow at the ready. I try a greeting and speak up but none of them answer, then I can't think of another word, the boy having come out of the same dusk singing opera, with a fish on a hook.

He stops, looking at the arrow now lifted at me.

It is he who remembers their song, who changes the opera into theirs, a song I repeated long ago when I danced for them. I must've sung it to him in the cradle. By the time he finishes singing it to the brave standing there, the others, who have taken the beef jerky and bullets, having tossed aside the silk, the others are listening too.

The arrow starts jigging with laughter. All the Indians laugh the way they used to hearing my song, they point at the boy and laugh, slapping the sides of their faces, their hands together.

The boy stops singing, the boy senses the song's meaning and stops.

All those many times I sang it for them and I didn't know its true meaning. I am old enough now, and I blush.

Well done, says one of them in good English, the one with the bow, which he lowers with another laugh. He gives the boy the hide bag that the Indian wears around his waist in payment for the provisions the other Indians walk away with. After they go, he slips his arrow into its hide holder and leans toward me, and my still flour-dusted hands, and says: Beware women.

Then a gun goes off down the street.

The last Indian flees as if he is smoke itself.

It is Henry's shot. He waits until the Indians are clear of the place, then, proud to have routed them, comes to waggle his service gun inside my store. I wanted to flush them, not catch you in amongst them.

They're gone all right, I say, backing away from the sulfur smell of the report. I leave them alone and we get along fine. What I wanted to know was what they meant about the warning they gave me—Beware women.

He meant, *Be careful, lady, or we'll get you next time*, says Henry. We have to convince the town to post a watch for Indians like them who are after ladies. Them Indians got their hands on ammunition, didn't they?

Probably for buffalo, I say. It wasn't much they bought.

No matter, says Henry. It's the sighting of them that matters. We don't have our share of turmoil and trouble now that the war is over so no fort is going to send us guards.

He rouses lookouts, three men with not enough to do waiting for harvest, him being one of them. They demand chairs and shade, otherwise, they say, it is a punishment not duty we are in the throes of, and duly they set up at three corners of the town, with one side the river. By the afternoon they are too sleepy to gossip with their few passersby, although one does catch the widow woman taking a side road with the blacksmith and manages to keep alert for another five minutes. It is hot and dry here, and the horizon is flat without the frill of landscape, just that tree in the far distance. The chance of anyone other than an Indian getting by is slim. Fear of this is mustered all around the town by the heroic guards but after that first fear fades, sleep fills them, sleep is what they fight.

Women bring food to where the guards sit, always hungry, gun-polishing and tobacco spitting, mending harness or keeping an hour's watch over a baby. I come out to join in the chorus of what a good job they are doing, there's not an Indian in sight, but by noon the second day, the men start insisting they have livestock to shoe, they have weeds waiting for them, they know how to kill the plague beetle with jars but they need to catch them to prove it. Most of all, the harvest has to come in soon or the weather will take it. They are far enough away from the Indian wars, they say, and Henry suggests they put the boy at the west end and have him bang two kettles together if he sees more Indians.

Go ahead, I tell the boy. You have to, or it won't be just the Indians taking you away.

He sits and sighs. There's plenty of thatching for him to work on. Though he doesn't say a word the whole time, that doesn't mean he won't. In that, he's like an Indian and maybe could sense them coming, I tell the women who circle with questions he won't answer like, What is your favorite opera song?

The harvest is hardly sheaved a week later when the woman from the committee for the dumb place comes marching over herself with her prayer book open, and five women as witnesses follow along behind her. Later I hear that they ask him first if he hears anything out of my cellar. He doesn't answer their question for a while, which gets them to tapping their feet the way they do, and then he says, Ghosts. They say *Ghosts?* real interested. He doesn't say anything again for a long stretch until they put this corkscrewed question about my cellar again to him, with the ghosts put into it casually, like that's about what you'd expect of my cellar, and his silence. He finally answers with, Yessirree, vegetable ghosts, dead turnips. Then he starts in on the whole of the Lord's Prayer as if he has been waiting all of his life for this chance to say it, and that is the end of them and their committee. The money for him they say they are putting in a fund for old maids, sly as they are about me.

I am kneading another ball of dough and the boy, relieved of his watch in recompense for his speech, is unraveling the worsted so we can sell it by the yard. His cat, usually so busy with the small varmints, tangles her paw in the yarn tail which gets the boy laughing, not speaking, no, he hasn't spoken a word more than he must since being forced, when a whole troupe of women—four of them—ride up to the river, all a-lather, their horses' mouths boiling.

I am staring so hard out the window I knead my knuckles under. The bonnets on the women sit deep, the way you wear them in dust or bad sun—the way I used to at the Indian's. When one of them swings herself down, I admire her for the way, with an old-fashioned bonnet like that, she doesn't hesitate or stop half down for footing but takes a stride right off the horse. But then she trips and falls flat to her face.

Begging your pardon, miss, she says to me, her skirts gathered.

Her voice is a whistle and a growl together, and she ducks her head so her face is still hidden in the bonnet.

The boy winds the worsted faster. The woman clears her throat and spits. Can I help? I ask.

We're hungry and in a hurry, she says, and makes a kind of curtsy.

Now women do not curtsy to each other. That's another thing. And this one is wearing a man's boots—though women will wear a man's boots too, sometimes, there's a class of women who must wear them to the field. But those ugly wide bonnets! No woman wears them now if she can help it.

I tell the boy to get the soup in the kettle for the ladies. To ladle it up, they're in a big hurry, judging by those lathered-up horses. They let the horses suck at the river like it is flowing one way into them, they cinch saddles and hitch up skirts. I am happy they don't bother the orchard with its walnut-big fruit.

We have a sick sister, says the woman in a squeak while I rough the bread dough off my hands. Half of the squeak she has stays low in the throat. We have to get her to the border where she has kin. The border is what we aim for, says the woman, nodding her head toward the others. We're much obliged for your help on where we can ride to meet it.

The others approach my kitchen, one tripping on a dress hem with his boot because now, seeing them closer, with their hands coming out of the bottom of the dress sleeves—nice plaids—I can see how hairy those hands are, and worn where a woman's wouldn't be, and how their rifles are bound in bundles of cornstalks to their stirrups, though they are trying to keep that side of the horses facing away from me, and how one of the horses shows black spots coming off that are painted on. I've been kept by Indians long enough to know how to hide fear, which is what I do while they take up the soup spoons my boy brings with the soup. I consider the Indian who warned me about women, my fort time in amongst the idle soldiers, and the two half-soldiers who stole the black horse so long ago in their big hurry while the ladies keep a ways off my store back.

Swallowing, all of them, inside their soup-stained bonnets.

The state border is just west of that rise out past town, I tell them. Keep to the rise, I say. There is a slight curve that will tempt you elsewhere, to the left of where the sun goes down. Good day, I say when the boy is back inside with all the bowls, and then I close the door on them.

We lie flat to the floor, and gauge the men's hesitation, their low talk of what to do about what they think I know. We lie in that quiet way until we hear the horses leave fast, until we hear the horses no more.

Those women, says the boy. They sure can ride.

I say to everyone, Did you see them? Everyone in town laughs and tells me I'm crazy, men who dress up like women? Men who dress up like women dangerous? Women like to ride hard when they will, and God bless them, says a man whose cuffs I turn. I chew at the pins in my mouth, saying no more.

Not a week later I am reading this sign on the old pony express wall:

> *Possessing as it does a soil unsurpassed in fertility, as the immense yields of grain in the past season attest and also a climate for healthfulness and purity clearly indicated by the bright eye of the toiler, the blooming freshness of our ladies, putting to shame the tawdry adornment of cosmetics and pearl paste . . .*

and commenting to the telegrapher that it is a good example of the fine words the homesteaders have been taken in by, and I even steal a piece of charcoal from the stove to underline the word "paste" where someone has written *Let's have some* when I spot a handbill adrift on his desk, a sketch of a homely whiskered desperado. There are four in his gang, it says in the written description. They kill and will kill again, it says in big letters. They are wanted for the latest in robberies, the ones on the new trains that are coming. They were all wanted weeks before.

It's them, I can't help but say. The women. I point at the sketch and description.

Sure enough, ma'am, says the telegrapher, yawning.

Shaved, who would he be? says a stagecoach handler who's loitering, gulping water. Your mother?

Everyone knows my story. They think I want a man so much I see them in women.

I should be happy the gang didn't kill me, and not care if anyone believes me. Instead I'm happy to see they are real, that I didn't imagine them like the townspeople insist. I did see them and so did the boy. Some days when the locals ridicule me about it, I wish I had ridden off with those men-women. Am I a Sister of Mercy, or one of so many girls all in a row, unmarried and saucy, scorning the labor of the wedded? Or younger, with braided hair at a river doing everyone's washing, or one of the outlaws' own sisters sick unto death, pale as ivory tulle, awaiting their big arrival? Or maybe I'm just a mean old woman with a tongue-stopped boy, wrinkled-red, seated on a rocker and inveigling mean sympathy.

No.

Chapter 22

The blanket-clad hunched-over shuffler is no worn Indian woman carrying a babe too weak to suck. He is the driven-off Indian, the one who tells the others that the mound will protect them, then the cavalry drags their cannon to the top of it and fires grapeshot into the village. The other Indians pick up stones, even William the Hat picks up these stones—not so much stones but what is left after the cavalry dynamites the side of the mound, blowing bone and locket, sand and clay and snake all the way to the river, trying to blow away that faith the cavalry assumes the Indians have found in it of themselves—and drive the Indian away.

There is nothing worse for an Indian than being driven off but right away, he tries to get a worn Indian woman carrying a babe too weak to suck to rebuild the mound for him. He has to build it all over as soon as he can. The Indians rain stones on him again to keep him from cajoling the woman into helping him rebuild, they say the cavalry will blow them all up next. The cavalry wants only to blow me up he says, with blood running from where it shouldn't, but the Indians know better, they know no one wants just one of anything.

Before William the Hat signals *Go* to the ponies dragging

what belongings are left to someone's uncle's half-brother's canyon, he pulls the Indian out of the mound rubble where he still sits surprised at being driven off, and tells him where he can flee to. William the Hat has heard about where from a runaway who hid with the Indians, pretending to be them. The cavalry will not think the Indian will pretend to be a slave and hide, especially with the slave's freedom now given. I know this is not the Indian way, says William the Hat, but you will find ways to make it Indian.

Stoning, always the stoning, the Indian says. He rubs at a wound on his head.

William the Hat will fetch him later, when the cavalry is not looking, the cavalry who says they want the snake-maker, they want to hang him by his feet and make him writhe.

It is hardly four days more that the Indian is slapping his good horse free beside the night-dark river. The good horse watches him wriggle into an opening, the place of entry not hard to find for an Indian, being among the bushes and the cleft of the riverside. When the Indian is at last hunched in the near dark of that cave beside the door into the cellar, he inspects the ledges hollowed out for sleep and seating. On one of them he finds some bones that a slave has left behind in a basket, the bones of someone loved. He turns them over and over. He is unable to sit quiet and hide beside these bones, he scratches a snake into the dirt in the side of the cave with one of them. These bones are a warning, a summons. He must build a mound for them, even if this mound is underground. What else does he know, in his craziness, in his life, but the mound? He must fetch water and dig and mound up the diggings over these bones along the length of the floor where he buries them, making its head beside the ledges where it's more open, the tail and rattlers at the cliff. It is the Indian way, it is his way.

At first he uses the bowl he finds left for the runaways, he uses that and his hands to carry the water from the river in the dark of the night to soften the dirt, and keeps his knife for digging. But that is too tiring. He is not used to this work. How can he make a mound all alone with just a bowl and a knife, without a woman? He knows he should stay where he is for such a time as he must and be quiet, but on the third night he steals into the store and locates the shovelhead beside the fireplace, and moves it slowly, so quietly from the grate—

I hold the gun on him, the one I have in safekeeping for the veteran. In this dark he is mostly smell, the familiar smell of the Indians who warned me about the women. I touch his arm with the gun. He shows his face in as much moonlight as he has chosen in this part of the house to avoid.

You! I say.

He is crazy, crazy. His eyes move wild, like an animal in a trap. With his free hand, he grabs the candelabra sitting on the table and bares his teeth.

Harriet, the boy calls out from his cot.

One of those drunks from the saloon got into the shop is all, I say. Go back to sleep, I say into the listening quiet.

Fear is what I should have, all the settlers have been working this fear on each other for some time now. That is how I found the gun so fast, with what fear they have given me. And I have feared him, yes I have, in my life beside the mound. But now I see the stiff way he holds his head, his thin face, his wounds sticky with sickness.

I suppose it is your horse I caught a few days ago, I say.

He could lift my hair off my neck and work a knife under

my scalp easy enough. I don't see a knife but he could still have one. But he could have done that earlier, when he first heard me shuffle in the dark, fetching the gun.

My slave, he says in his language. He releases the candelabra.

It is too dark to figure out more in languages who remembers, especially with such fear, fear that mounts and makes our hearts beat alike—hard and loud.

He says in Indian that he needs this—he points to the shovelhead. Or you, he says, my slave from before.

It takes me time to work out all those words. He repeats them twice, slow, tapping the shovelhead.

I might be a different person now, I say back. If I weren't so lame.

I hold the gun steady. I take a step back to show I can improve my aim.

The Indian says you move like my second wife who died when the cavalry shot at the mound with their cannons. The way you move, he says with a grunt.

This has always worked with women before.

You think I have to keep you? I say. That you have claimed me? He could so easily twist the long barrel from my hands, but instead he twists his head, he twists it away from me.

I understand this to mean *I have no choice*. I do not pull the trigger but I do not turn away. I point to the rug in disarray over the cellar hatch. Go back down.

He tucks the shovelhead under his arm. I don't stop him. He swings himself into the cellar, eyes quick on me, then off.

I hear him digging again in the time it takes for me to breathe, the digging I was sure before was an animal's. I lean the gun against the wall and shake out my hands. I am crying. I use my sleeve to catch the wetness.

It is an exchange that will never right itself—all the father I have now digs below me. I have nothing else. Every winter when I chop ice out of the river, my worst chore, I see otters swimming under the shelf and dream about wearing a pelt coat made of those he trapped, the closest I can get to his own skin, but I don't have even a scrap. Just this Indian. He knew my father, the Indian was his friend, and now I harbor him.

I leave bread and the jam he used to give us before the dances, and whatever I find that Indians eat, jerky and the tail end of a squash I save out as if I am going to eat it myself later. I tell the boy nothing. We each have our own fears, not the settlers'. What will the town do if the boy tells? The lieutenant coming through town put the head of an Indian on the bedstead of his twin boys, someone's hawking an Indian skull for $1.25 suitable for reduction into ladies' combs, and no one took down a hung Indian in the town center for days, an Indian who used the wrong word in English to a woman. To sit in the dark alone as no Indian or human should is heinous punishment in itself. To top that, the cavalry bugles while its rigs rattle on the street so close the Indian can hear every day how happy they are with their Indian war.

The horse he brought is a good one.

There, in his head, under his hair against the cellar dirt over him, the Indian sees, with the help of the little food she leaves—does she think he will eat her stores through?—he sees people in the dark—very dark people, very very dark people—and one white, the leader Tall Hat, the one the railroad took across the land as a corpse so he knows for sure it is not Tall Hat alive but someone in his head like the others. This Tall Hat takes off his hat and from inside its tall stovepipe blackness, he brings out a paper. William the Hat told him that Tall Hat's grandfather was killed by an Indian watching him railsplitting, someone who saw that these rails would keep the Indian horses from passing, and of course the buffalo from pastureland. Even the buffalo Tall Hat would keep from us. The Indian dreams William the Hat sits down here in this dark place with him, a place so much like the mound on the inside except of course he never went inside it, only his dead slave women did. William the Hat always knew about dreams. It was William the Hat who sat beside the fire, his eyes half closed, and told him that Indian blood is fixed to Tall Hat's Homestead Act. Tall Hat is for the railroaders. Even while Tall Hat's war is killing both sides of his people, he said, Tall Hat sees us as worse. Hearing about that Act, William the Hat took off his hat and burnt it. Oh, the smell, he said. Like a wet hide on an inside fire in winter. William told everyone to call him Bare Head afterward but no one would. He had worn that hat.

The only good Indian is dead, William the Hat said he heard. He said Tall Hat's whole-city-burning general said that even before that war of theirs was finished. Oh, the Indian heard about that good Indian well enough, from William the Hat and then others. While the telegraph birds sang and the buffalo scratched the poles for pleasure, this message spread everywhere.

Tall Hat has dipped his hand into the black hole of his hat and removed a paper.

Words on paper are snakes. You go for the tail to keep

them from making their way into the sand and then the tail is gone before your foot lands. Snakes are good for mounds but not for paper. William the Hat disagreed, said the letters are like the little horses or shields or arrows we put on hide that are caught. But Tall Hat's words on paper can't be caught. Maniacs or wild beasts? is what is written on this paper about the Indians. In his head, freedom is only for people who have been brought here in boats.

He hits his own head so hard against the ground above him that dust covers the beads on his chest, the ones he had to sew to the deerskin himself when his wives were very hungry and said having to feed those who built the mound made them hungrier. Did he give them food? He made himself more handsome.

He brushes the dust away from his beads with his shaky hand. It is time for William the Hat to find him.

Chapter 23

The peddler's new pipe-smoking self clambers down from his rig with a cough. I will convince you to take a few of these new pipes, he says, people will want them now that they're all back from their war, to smoke up their savings. One whiff of this new Virginia tobacco, and every pipe will be gone. The peddler has put on weight in the half year he's traversed his loop this time, and he bangs open the door with a behind as big as the case of pipes his short arms grip.

Wait for me here, I say. I slap my *No Trade Return Soon* sign into my window. I have to run get a cure for fleas from a woman up the way. I hold my hand out for the pipe case. You didn't bring any cures, did you?

I have nothing in the way of cures for insects, he says. I sold all my best stock last week to an undertaker. *Oy geveldt*, what is such a person going to do with good poison, with all those cadavers?

He sucks his new pipe red so I will notice it but I am distracted. I shove my restock list at him in haste. How I am suffering, I say and I pull up my skirts, revealing both my good and bad ankle, one he can see has been rubbed red-raw even through the thin white cotton hose he sold me two visits earlier, at such a discount.

The peddler scuffles away from those ankles, good or bad, alarmed at the provocation. Poison is what you need.

It's the boy I worry over, I tell him. The boy scratches until he bleeds. I've tied gloves on him at night to keep him from getting at the gallinippers and he still opens the sores in his sleep. I won't be but a minute riding over for the remedy.

The peddler has already heard about my horse. Since it came into my ownership without him, it doesn't exist for him, though I claimed it and trained it myself. The horse is the primary cause of your infestation is what he would say, if anything.

He does not even comment on its hello whinny.

I trot off with the boy in the saddle behind me, the boy who wants the brief company of the neighbor's boy more than a cure, and especially their new puppy, perhaps the true flea carrier now that our cat ran off. Once we are gone, the peddler should be off plying his trade down the street or unpacking at the new hotel, wasting no time, but while squeezing his load of pipes back onto his trap, minus my lot, he recalls the cure he tells me about later: the sulfur candle, one a charlatan from Charlotte gave him to try but he hadn't yet, there being no fleas for an itinerant peddler to battle except for the ones he might collect when he stops for the ladies and their pocketbooks.

Opportunity has its way of presenting itself.

He withdraws the candle from a fat satchel, finds the rock I use to wedge closed the door, secures the candle level to it by means of its dripped wax, and rights it, lit and smoky. A nice yellow smoke. He closes my windows and opens the door between rooms. Anticipating a bout of congratulations from my lips, and the possibility of a good fee, he pushes aside my rug, opens the hatch, and eases his bottom down into the cellar with his lit smoky candle, but hears what halfway down? A haunt left from the slave-time? Or a rat? He has it on common knowledge—his own—that former fugitives now prefer the hotel, they are getting so wealthy.

A rat would just as well be rid of as a flea with what he has planned.

He beats up a high thick stink of smoke in the cramped cellar, one sure to pour through the floorboards and wisp into the room beyond. There's no fire possible—he makes sure of that, he tells me later, not with the rock at the base of the candle. He starts to cough but makes certain the candle is still burning well before he stumbles back up the stairs.

Soon a yellow smoke-curl escapes along the hatch cover. After an hour—no fleas, no rats. Maybe a smoky trace in the velvets will remind the customers of eggs and ham, a sure sale. He shuts the doors tight as he leaves, then lean against his trap, all smiles, awaiting my return. He will ask just a small amount for such a fine exercise of his wits.

No fleas! I shriek. I do shriek. He is holding his hand out, it lies flat readied for payment, but when I make that shriek, the hand flies to his ears, he pulls up his shoulders to protect those ears, he retracts his *Thank Me* face under his flat black hat. I shriek about the smoke that lies thick as cloth outside and inside my house then I turn on him with *Skedaddle*! Blinking, he heaves his big-bottomed self back into his cab, mounts it like a man one hundred pounds lighter and whips his horse off so fast one of the ladies waiting for him with a special order loses her hat in his passing.

I slap a wet rag over my face and fling the windows open. I tell the boy to stay outside while the house airs, that I am going to look for preserves broken by the heat. The boy is already pulling off his gloves to scratch.

The search is a turn of my head, the cellar's room is that small.

Sleeping beside the Indian's fires allows me to see better than most through this smoke, even if it ruins the everyday sight, and there's a singed light from between the floorboards overhead. I wave my arms at the haze and work the false cupboard back with my free hand. The passage beyond the room is dead black with smoke. I should have brought a lamp or a candle and not relied on my Indian eyes. I cough into the rag over my face and step along the passage. The ground's uneven, I trip where disturbed earth's piled up in the middle, piled higher than need be.

Even in such dark, I know a mound, its smoothed sides, its packed top.

I move around it, sidling to where sand and rock and dirt cave in over it, I limp to where I feel—

—his skin, a cold arm where it lies against the cave-in.

My fingers find his face where it's pressed against a crack of air.

Out—he couldn't get out. Who closed the cave?

I cough into the rag. I cough again.

The town would congratulate me if I dragged him out and presented him dead. But he's more human than most, than many of the townspeople. I drag his body into the ditch he's made for digging the earth for the mound, then I beat on the mound until it gives up chunks. I go wild with my beating. Destroy—I destroy it. No mounds for remembering, no memory. I must bury him in it to hide him, to have him forgotten. I must forget him myself, the way I have Pa. In my destroying and burying, I find the bones he has dug in already, and that is when I call on his god—Look down, God—you remember them all for us.

I bury him under the broken clay and bones and sand as best I can and I jam the door to the passage closed.

The smell will be a dead rat's.

Chapter 24

I found mushrooms down there, I say. That's what took all the time. I stretch out my hand full of the pale smoky fruit.

If the floor is dirt, some find mushrooms at their feet every morning. The boy hardly looks up from teasing a smoke-silly fly. You been down there too long.

I wash my hands and face, I wash and I wash. The basin is black when I am finished, the towel blacker. The boy is watching me so close that I start to tell him that it is dangerous in the cellar now, he should not come down and bother it, not even for his spoonfuls of jam, the smoke is still so bad and you know how the supports need strengthening, and he says, The smoke got him?

I hold still then. You been down there?

He shrugs as if down there is just anybody's cellar. I liked having my own Indian.

He was his own Indian, I say. Nothing else going down there now, just jam, you hear?

The boy is giving me his side-eyes but he can see I am stern and unwilling to take back-sass. I hug him even if he doesn't want hugging, even if he struggles free.

Henry's mother bangs open the store door just then with

a *Yoo-hoo* and a *I can tell you're burning sulfur* and a *Don't lift a finger I'll be right there*, and in the time it takes for me to ball up the dirty towel, she walks right around to where we stand.

I aim to hand over the seventy-five cents we owe on the suit Henry wore to the picnic, she starts off saying with her face at a sour angle, which means, for her, a smile. She holds the sum out and then steps back. *Gott in Himmel*. You Bohemians, she says after a long indrawn breath. Don't you know them mushrooms grow in clefts that the dead like?

They are good to eat, I say.

We three look at the plate they now sit on.

I suppose you grow them in your cellar? says the woman. Henry wonders what else you got down there. Wine in bottles? She lifts her skirts as if wine is about to wash over her feet and pollute them. I hate to mention this, I am not the smelling committee, but it does stink bad of sulfur everywhere.

Rotten eggs, the boy says.

I don't have a single flea, I say, smoothing my apron with clean hands. Thanks to the peddler.

That peddler is good for something. She watches me wipe my sore eyes with an apron tail. You seen Henry yet? He's supposed to meet me here for his fitting.

Not a hair of him.

The boy yawns at this talk, the boy plays tiddly with a cat's cradle.

The old woman shakes her head. Henry, she says. I don't know what about Henry any more. He's gotten so peculiar and—

She doesn't finish. Instead she lays out a pair of men's pants on the table. I've got to have these widened, she says. He is getting back to his real weight at last. They called them blue-bellied Yankees but there warn't much belly to them after they finished with all their marching. And here—

Out of the same satchel she pulls a lump wrapped in a cloth. The cloth falls open or she pulls it open—it is all in the same motion—and a cake slice reveals itself. I hope you'll find the time to do the pants, she says to me, pointing at the cake.

The cake steams hot as if it is molten gold. Oh, time, I say.

She slaps the boy's hand before he pounces.

Run fetch a plate, she says to him. Be polite. Say, she says, I got me some fleas too. It's the season. Didn't the peddler leave supplies of what he used on your cellar?

Nothing, I say. He didn't leave anything.

The boy levers the cake from the cloth onto the plate, the left crumbs brushed to his palm.

You are a quiet one like they say, says the woman. But I know boys. You'll grow talkative and tall soon enough. The woman steps back toward the door, then cranks her head forward. Maybe he's a little smoke-afflicted too. Tell me, you a flea?

He looks away.

Henry will show up soon, she says, I'll make sure he does.

My shoulders shake a little after the door closes and the boy notices, enough so he snatches at the cake for more than a taste.

Chapter 25

The crime of immigrants is how people freely—most of them—leave their families, their very countries, and settle elsewhere, never returning again for the rest of their born days, says Henry.

I am stacking bolts in the back, only half-listening. Henry is flirting, bringing up family. The mention of family is as close as he can get to courting. He orates on a fruit box while below him the boy whistles opera, chalking Henry's pants in light-fingered boredom. Before the boy learned how to measure this seam so close to a man's part, I had to guess and make do. Handy, this boy—add a few more chores and he will make himself half partner, someone I might need with business getting so good, especially with Henry.

For the last two weeks Henry has called on me *la-di-dah* for this and that. His mother has blessed and abetted his calling not only by bringing in his old pants for new seams but earlier, by buying a navy checked dress length so woebegone from light from the shop window even I thought it was plain white. That is what she owed the seventy-five cents on, not the pants I sewed up for a piece of cake.

If I take Henry seriously, I won't get cake anymore is how I see it.

No one thought immigration was a crime when it came to where the Indians would live, I say, coming back out when the boy's whistling changes after the chalk work is over.

Indians is another story. We moved them, they did not move themselves voluntary. He strokes the pair of pale muttonchops that widen his face. Harry—for he calls me Harry—did you know that Indians will chew and swallow human bones if they have to?

The boy's opera stops altogether.

You had better believe it, he says, stepping off the fruit box with a jig so his pants hang straight, then pointing at the boy. And the Indians will come and get you next time.

They have come in the past, says the boy. They were customers.

I marvel at his snap.

Indians will not be customers in the future, says Henry. He works his face in a serious way then fishes a pickle of out my barrel. I paid a dime for ten of these last week, he says, and I haven't collected on the tenth. He pops it whole onto his upper lip like a mustache and wiggles it, then drops it into his mouth.

My boy can't help but laugh.

I laugh too, despite his Indian talk. Knowing his old unsad self, the town and his mother have rubbed away the war in him, expecting his pranks of wire birds flapping in the outhouse, his General Grant pretend-stagger, and now this pickle trick—why, he's almost a Henry a person could hope to change. Here's the work your mother wants, I say.

Other mothers send their sons in for thimbles impossibly

small or special washing soap shelved high so the son will see my ankles, or have the boys wait while I measure their corsets, bone by bone, or bother me while I count my stacks. Other mothers compliment me on my walk, my back so set straight despite my limp, but none of the sons return on their own, just the old bent men huddled around the store stove, going on about how many fat cows I might wish I shared with them, then promising to take my boy out to hunt.

I would take him myself but I have the store to mind.

Those younger men can't abide my store-mongering, my having no time to compose the simpers they expect. Nor can they stomach my needing so few of their efforts. Henry's not so old that he thinks with his whiskers, but not so young that he talks all foolishness. Or is he just greedy like the others, wanting me for my pickles?

He accepts his mother's trumped-up sewing. How about honey for payment? he asks, and he lifts the corner of his shirt to show me his bee stings. Gathering honey, his latest financial scheme, gives him the means to prove both the strength of his bees and himself. They're not even sore, he says, touching one of the welts on his chest. I used the horse liniment you sold Ma in the spring and rubbed it in good. He pretends it's everyday, this showing me his bare skin.

Six jars of honey on the shelf, I say. I don't need any more. I collect the new-chalked pants from the boy, who's just standing there, watching Henry cavort.

Henry, the bee-loving pickle thief, must be watched.

The new bank will sure be glad to see this pair of pants finished, I say.

The bank, he sighs, twirling a loose button on its side

across the counter. Tomorrow I will make my presence known well enough in the new bank. The button falls. All in a rush he says, Is there a length good enough a match to the checked one that Ma bought that she might want another for her birthday? He points into the back where the bolts lie.

Could be, but—I don't fall for his ploy of pawing through the lengths with him. Who knows what he wants?

The boy whistles and wanders off.

But I'm not one to lose a sale if there's one to be plucked, even one as dubious as this, so I nab the first navy worsted I see and quote him a price out of the air. Without a second of hesitation, he produces the bills and a few loose coins that I know altogether is his whole pay for scything wheat this week. Very nice, he says.

When our hands touch over the money, the room fills with his desire—even I can feel it—while outside from where the boy has gone comes his opera whistle over and over, those few first notes stopped, as if nothing more will ever happen.

Before I cut the lengths, I say, more to break this ricochet of feeling than to jinx the sale, I think your mother needs a set of soup spoons more.

Oh? he says in a kind of stopped-dream surprise.

I bring him one.

These are too high-priced and you know it, he says, tapping the spoon bowl into his palm. He's smiling foolishly, and wipes the cabinet front with his free finger as if it is dusty and not polished daily. But might you be selling some of those better rings?

Your mother has the notion for a ring?

Let me see the rings, he says, and he pets those mutton-chops of his again.

I finger my key set to the cabinet for the smallest, the one hardest to work.

Except for the blisters and the hard parts, you have nice hands, he says, one eye lifted as if my fingers tangled around the keys were horse's teeth being decided upon.

I am used to labor, I tell him. I fumble and fit the lock at last.

My mother says you like work, he says. She says she never saw a woman more fresh from it.

Set in the tray, the rings I bring out shine like so much tinsel.

Pretty enough is what Henry calls them.

The most popular are gone, I say, the Ivy Entwined with the sapphire chip. The Mauer girls took the two I had for their double engagement. I tap the tray. If you see one that is smaller around than you need, you can always get the smith to beat it bigger.

He asks the name of each stone but in the end he selects a ring by price. It doesn't take him long. Only one is worth more than the others, a tiny ruby set in a gold heart-shape.

Put it on, he insists. I want to see it on so I can decide.

Henry is sly enough, but not at all rich—this I know, and feel his mother's breath inhaled, and also know other girls don't limp.

I make a kind of up and down laugh.

Come on—your hand—he insists.

But the blisters, I say. I won't be able to take it off.

Oh, one of your salves will work quick enough, he says and roughly pushes the ring over the finger. His own fingers shake, which explains the roughness but not the why.

I hold out my hand, I model the ring and stare at him over the fingers.

Of course I will take on the boy, he says. He aims a big grin at me, all a-jitter. He's never had a real refusal of any kind from a woman is what I suspect, at least not from his mother, and she does count.

It will take time to get the ring off and time is not on my side.

I touch the jewel. I press the hand with the ring on it to a spot just between my breasts, I find my declaration, I give him my full affirmation, I say Yes.

Chapter 26

Where that tree pulls the river up and I left the balloonists behind so many years before, is where picnics are taken now and buggies disappear to and more than one red-faced local walks back from, without his shoes. Once I heard about a girl in a state of having drunk too much who let boys tie her corset laces to two different horses standing there. She was lucky to live. Whenever the water gets low, broken wagon wheels and tossed-out cook stoves and other such trash no one has any use for anymore stick up right at that spot is what Henry points out.

It'll cost the railroad plenty to make the curve to miss it, he says to his friend who comes with us for the wet-nosed neighbors' sake. The boy comes too, for his own. This taking me out in a buggy to the river is altogether an afterthought, what a man might do to clinch the deal, since he has already sent word to the priest.

Henry's friend, a man full of opinions gathered while he stayed out of the war doing the yeoman's job of replacing the sons and brothers in the field but on account of that, afraid of anyone not already known to him or those sons and brothers, asks, Do they really want the train bringing in all these different kinds of people? People ride in on the coach and they're trouble already, thieves and strangers, he says.

New customers, I say. People who don't already owe me money.

The two men laugh. The boy pulls out a hook and line he plans to drag through the river's start, and he twirls it, waiting to be released from the buggy.

I heard the trains might kill livestock too, says Henry. If I had cows, I'd think about fencing, and that new barbed wire to boot.

To boot? says his friend.

The war taught me that, laughs Henry. And there's absquatulate.

Haven't heard that one, I say.

A fancy word for "Take your leave." Skedaddle.

We disembark.

Whatever else the war taught him his face doesn't always cover. He's a curious one, and I can't say I know much more about him than what his mother mentions in her everyday visits that I don't half hear anymore, glorying in the condition of the premarital where every word is a thank you. Time is what stretches itself in front of us, lots of married-in-the-future time to work out such secrets.

Today I'm in no shape to ask questions anyway, I harbor a well-along cold. It is part of our courtship that I endure the cold for a chance at an outing together, the men's talk and their cuffing, along with bringing the smoked meat and all the trimmings. I am not used to keeping company at length with anyone other than the boy. At least his friend brings along a little liquor. It's not that I'm partial but it helps me breathe. About all that keeps me upright is Henry, sneaking his arm around my waist, which, without my malady, he wouldn't dare try.

His friend and the boy go fetch brush for firewood while Henry lifts me and the basket and the sundries out of the buggy. Henry has brought wheat rolls he says he made himself before dawn and I tend to believe him, given his boasting about himself as Old Tar and his cook's time in the cavalry, and the way he showed me how to spread fish skin over a cup to filter coffee. While he smooths a blanket over the tufted dry grass that fall leaves, I touch the cold water over the clay bottom and then Henry touches it too, and the river ripples.

In the quiet, Henry says, It's smooth as a snake, and draws his finger through the water in an S.

I blow my nose. Did you ever see the Indian's mound before it was shot at? It had a snake-shape.

You are real sweet on Indians, says Henry.

They are like trees, they are part of the land. There are other people like that, trappers, for one.

I watch him.

He dries his hands on his pants. Trees are darned dangerous if you ask me, he says. Shakespeare had them trees in one of his plays that snuck up.

Henry's friend drops some old branches in front of us. You don't believe what they talk about in those plays, do you?

Henry smiles and shakes his head No, then breaks up the branches with his feet. He says the train's the real snake in this country, following the river like it knows its own mind. It's coming to get us all. I hear there's only forty miles between us, and the last rails. Soon there will be nowhere to hide after the train comes.

Who wants to hide? asks the boy.

I mean, a place for a soul needing solace to find that is quiet, without the machinery of the modern age always pulling through. Not hide like a bear asleep, says Henry, stomping one last branch to bits.

There's talk of moving the capital of the country all the way out here, right dead center, says his friend. You could do it with the train, have the senators live in soddies with carpets from Persia on the floor. Everyone would gravitate here.

You are train-crazy, says Henry. Like all of them.

Henry's friend laughs and produces a ball from the trap to toss to the boy, who does not like to catch, and he doesn't. A lot of larks sitting on the river look around and fly off when Henry's friend flings out his arm like he's going to throw the ball at them too. His own girl has what I have, a darned bad cold, only her mother keeps her covered in plasters and at home. She has sent the boiled eggs.

After we eat, Henry helps me back into the buggy where I can rest my head, and he and his friend sit nearby burning the broken branches and talk about a kind of soft wheat he has heard about, one that grinds easier. With the train, it's bound to come, I hear his friend say and Henry says if it comes, he'll plant it.

I don't lean out to correct him, saying you don't have anywhere to plant, I don't say I heard your brother took all the family land while you were out soldiering, or even that you should homestead your own land if you want your own wheat. No one brings up the new bank that took on the Binner widower instead of him. What I do say, as soon as his friend goes off to throw rocks in the river with the boy, who does like that kind of throwing, is that a cook like you might consider opening a café along the front side of the store, and for that, he steals a kiss. And then a second one.

It takes my breath away, as if two horses are tied to my corset strings.

I could do figures in the shop too, he tells me next, he is real handy with both the figures and the frying.

I don't know about that. I take a sip of the liquor and daub at my nose. Yesterday I cleared ten dollars, doing all the figuring.

He knows how well I do by myself. I can't find it in me to tell him I don't need him in the shop because I do, but this kind of need is so new I don't know quite what it is. I only know that I should speak low using my cold as an excuse when he comes near so he has to lean even closer, that is what the girls who get measured for their weddings tell each other to do when they think I am just pinning. He listens to me like a dog would, paws together, gazing at something else because my face is now too close to look at, he listens for a long time until his friend ventures up to the buggy and says, Henry, it's going to rain.

While his friend fixes the harness, I tell him about traveling here in a wagon after the boy's Pa and Ma died of lightning.

And a sister, says the boy, climbing in.

I didn't know about the sister, says Henry. My mother told me quite a bit.

The storm gets so bad, Henry's friend has to walk the horse part way back, it's skittish, and there's chill enough that Henry has to pull me closer.

Chapter 27

Mazel tov, growls the peddler. The glory of Henry's blue wedding suit worn every day, and the gold band on his finger the peddler brought to my door himself earns this begrudged exclamation. Henry does not understand it though or else he doesn't hear it. Perhaps the peddler has spat into his beard? Henry answers instead with She's busy in the stockroom, in the note of triumph that the newly wed make, having bliss as its basis. What have you got for us?

Go boil your shirt, says the peddler.

Instead of relieving Henry of the restocking list and pushing it close to his eyes where he sees best, the peddler steps back out onto the boardwalk and shouts: Come close, every *schmegegge* idiot in this town! You must hear! She stole this business out from under the shopkeeper the minute he was shot. From a dead man! She came here as a *gonif* and bewitched you all. You ought to be ashamed.

That so? passersby exclaim and nod. Other townspeople emerge in clumps from nearby stores to watch the peddler build in fury. It is enough like a natural disaster that the mothers cover the ears of children-in-arms and direct the ones who can walk to walk elsewhere. In the middle of the peddler's unreeling his rant, Henry opens the shop door just wide enough to pour a bucket of water over his head, then slams it shut before the peddler can belt him.

Shaking off water like a dog up and down the boardwalk, the peddler blusters and rants. Two of the other shopkeepers drag their faces off their window smears and come out of their shops to calm him. They take him and his big bags over to the hotel where he is bought a drink, and then another. He tells all that he knows to what is now quite a respectable crowd, a preposterous story about the girl working for an Indian and about how she came to be owner of the shopkeeper's goods and so rich. Absolutely! he tells them. They all nod and smile, they hear him out, then they refill his glass yet again, pleased with bearing possible superior knowledge to those who haven't heard every word, whether true or not, happy with any story told on a neighbor, especially one who has prospered. But to them it is more a story about him and a ruined romance. When someone asks when his mother is sending his own bride, a bride of his own true faith, he rages all the way out the door of the hotel, dragging his heavy bags with him, swearing on his mother's grave that he will never trade nothing—not a stick, not a stitch—in that town again.

But the town has heard him. The Indian story is not so far-fetched. They remember talk of an Indian going in and out of that cellar, carrying water. It is one of the neighbors who, aided and abetted by his fellow loungers, rolled a boulder over the opening to see if they could catch the Indian out. When nothing came of that plugging, the talk died down. Talk like the peddler's only convinces them that what I needed all along was someone to watch over me. A crazy peddler can't do that, wandering here and there, taking his time crossing the whole country. They wait a day until Henry laughs about the peddler's having a lost tribe of his own, and then they forget all about the man's rantings.

Have you ever been to Virginia? the boy asks Henry. The boy is still none too talkative at twelve, so little that he usually gets an answer back, even from Henry. This girl who is older than me in my school says Virginia is a place you would not forget.

Henry is slumped in the bath, washing out his ears with a rag so it takes him some time to clear his hearing to say he could have been to Virginia, the army didn't have signs around that said this hill or bush is Virginia. He did walk a lot of places, and once they all stood up in wagons and were pulled through the countryside as prisoners. He heard there was bad battling in Virginia and he flops his leg out of the tub and shows the boy a funny hole in his thigh that has healed over that he got in Ohio.

The boy puts his finger into that hole and Henry flinches. I can still feel it, he says. I forget a lot of things but this is the way a place like that stays with you.

The boy goes back to mending what Old Man Rains has taken to calling his last set of pants, he is that old, and says, You told me it was from Mississippi the last time.

Henry, I say. Which is it?

Henry touches that hole showing about an inch over the cooling-fast bathwater and closes his eyes.

Ha, says the boy. Talking.

Some mornings Henry's hot cakes don't flip back onto the griddle or his eggs break clean of their shells but he keeps on cooking anyway, sure, he says, that his war talents will show through soon enough. His mother has given me an antidote to indigestion she says works on his food and swears in the four years he was gone, she never ran out of his hardtack, she still chews on it, it is that unforgiving.

He is at his happiest stirring or chopping next to the stove, and then serving whatever results to customers on a bench just outside the door. What few of them give over money for his cooking are usually just passing through, people got up in the world enough not to have to pack beans in a saddlebag but still wanting something hot and easy for their wanderings without the cost of the hotel. One of these itinerants lingers too long over a bad plate of rabbit Henry has concocted out of water and potatoes and a small animal maybe more of a ground squirrel, and that one says, Henry, I know you.

Now I am out, bringing a specially sewn bandage to a man bitten on the nose by a skunk. Henry had wished me godspeed and what was that man doing smelling a skunk so close? Henry was supposed to go right off and measure the saloon for a mirror a man backed into too hard but these days he can't resist the cooking and the man who stopped couldn't resist the eating.

Or the speaking.

I am slow in my return as the bandage did not look like it would do the job, the nose being too big, all swollen up even when we wrapped it tight. By the time I walk in, Henry has taken flight, skipped, lit out with my horse, and left no note. Only this man who lingers over his bad rabbit has anything to say about what has gone on which is, That was the Henry who has the twin boys out in Eldridge, Missouri. I'd a known him anywhere with that kind of cooking.

I am carrying inside me at least a boy or a girl myself.

This lingering man doesn't seem to notice. He says, Can I have his old job? I can really cook.

Out, I say. Out of here.

Quick as anything, everyone in town has the knowledge I didn't, everyone. The man does not stop yapping about it his whole time here, exclaiming how the two boys look just like him doubled, how the mother wore the widow's weeds for a year after the list came out with him missing-in-action. He is from this woman's town, the wife's, that's how he knows everything. It is his very own town that now has a bigamist's wife.

Henry's mother says, Not my son. Henry's friend says maybe Henry didn't run, maybe he was killed by the man. What if the man killed him and buried him somewhere and the horse too, and made up the whole story after?

But Henry left before the man left, I say.

I know Henry the way his mother does not. All that sly pickle-on-the-lip charm doesn't account for his odd answerings, that hole-in-his-leg confused story, the way he shied away from some subjects with a sudden sadness. I did not ask him too many questions, for all the questions he did not ask me, especially after the peddler's talking to everyone.

I say we telegraph to the town the man's going on about and clear it up. After all, I say, this man who talks so much is a stranger to us, he could be just someone with a foul grudge.

I don't think the telegraph will tell you much more about him or where he is headed, the man tells me on my way to the office. He takes to following me, swearing all he says is true, on the Bible if I want. The wife with the twins is a harridan, he says. I seen her beat him about the ears with a broom once for tardiness. It was that kind of war he was in. He cashiered out. Now he will go all the way to California is what I think. There you could be married to two Chinese and enjoy it—begging your pardon, ma'am—and no one will look against you.

Or Utah, he adds. With them Latter Day Mormon people who like to double up anyway.

You got what you want from him, he says at the last.

I shrink my bulk in front to protect it, I pull my coat close.

The telegraph operator relays a Yes, there is a woman there, waiting for a man like that. He is sorry to deliver such a message, especially to me who found the notice of the men who dressed as women on his board that everyone laughed over but that turned out to be true, but he gets a lot of sad messages. At least no one is dead, he says.

The man stops following me and collects money from people who have bet I am honest, and money from the people who bet I am not, and leaves town before I find out who is who. Fury and sadness both is all that Henry gets from me after that. A man who could have used a woman like me and was too fearful to make it right—stupid.

Henry's mother twitters in confusion. One day she brings me all Henry's school papers, on another she takes his shirts back. She gets to feeling poor in the heart, she tells me, but won't take my cure, says she'd feel better off if she moved to a more agreeable climate. Maybe South. Maybe they will take her in Florida. There is lots of call for housework there in the big places they are building with the out-of-work slaves, she says, and she has a cousin who doesn't know about the bigamy. Oh, my Henry, she says, as if she could still fix him up. Then she is gone, just the way Henry went, in no time.

She can't stay for the baby.

The boy and I sit in the store like scabs, wondering. The boy has stopped whistling and his eyes switch away from my front like that too is an affront, which it is, but it is growing on me. It is growing. I stay as quiet as I can for all the rest of the months it waits to be born, right up until someone must be fetched. The boy fetches for me, then runs off at the release of my first real cry. He runs out to the river and it is a full day before I get him back.

That is not to say my cries don't reach the river.

Chapter 28

The boy can't get enough of the Chinese and Irish camp's rough strangeness, the men's noisy progress in their violent job of spiking the river's route with tracks. And standing beside the rails, he's not with the baby, who is such trouble to mind. No amount of threat or sweet talk from me teases him away, no scolding or promise of milk with a drop of sweet almond syrup. Between hay and grass is what that age is. He nods at me when I walk all the way out there to scold him, and then halfway home, he argues about the size of the baby's head or the number of birds in a flock, and wanders back. Only the promise of my cooking Henry's mother's cake can get him back to do the chores a minute before dark.

The Irish interest him more than the Chinese. He says they have the Chinese beat for size, it takes them three blows to drive a spike. Maybe the Chinese are weak from having to have their food shipped to them and it's old when they get it, he says. But their languages sound the same, squeaky and sputtered. His own talk triples with all the excitement, and he even learns a few of their songs in Irish or Chinese, who knows which, and sings the railroad songs they sing together in English to work harder. He tells me there is also one Bohemian man, very old, working for the railroad who pulls buffalo skins and tongues on a dray. He owns a pet buffalo that drinks beer, he's a man full of stories about wandering the countryside after real game, not just these few rabbits that are left. This Bohemian with a long stained mustache has eyes like you do, yes, that's about right, he says—or at least the eyes of all his friends. How many true Bohemians does he have for schoolmates? Marek, and one or two of the more square-jawed girls in his class of ten, quite a few. A hard bunch is what that Virginia girl calls them, and that is what she is going to write about after she moves, she tells him, all about their mulish obstinacy and arrogance. At least he is not Bohemian.

Where is the old man? I ask, patting the crying baby.

The boy shrugs. At the next town most likely, he says. He hasn't been around the dispatch point since last week. After the rails are laid, he adds, the men say they will take me on a trip.

I shush the baby.

The workers already let him ride the flat car to the end of the line and fetch water at one cent a bucket. He wouldn't go anywhere with them really, it would be just a trip to see where they plan to go.

The cake is on the sideboard, I say. I am going to go lay down with the baby for the time it takes to cool.

I lie beside the wriggly infant with my eyes wide open, soughing my best to suggest sleep. But I'm not sleeping. If that was Pa he met, what happened to those sisters of mine? Are they having their own children somewhere without me, are they familied-up altogether and not caring a whit? If Pa is an actual railroader, why doesn't he ask for me along the line?

I cannot abide a moment thinking Pa and my sisters are dead. I can bury the Indian but I can't bury them.

But if they are dead, I can forgive them their families, their not putting notices in papers for me like I did so often for them, their not searching and finding me.

I hug the baby too hard and she squawks, opening her eyes as wide as mine.

I guess he buys food from the workers with his one-cent water-hauling money, but it takes me weeks before I figure this out. When the boy eats none of the food I leave on a plate beside his bed, left for him like he lived at the bottom of the cellar, I tell him, We are going to take you to the phrenologist to feel your bumps and sort out why you aren't hungry since the everyday doctor didn't find anything wrong. I am about to take him to where the phrenologist holds his sessions, pull him by his ear across the town when the peddler shows.

The town has grown so quickly with the certainty of its railroad that he can't consider the loss of trade any longer, or so he says to the crowd at his heels. He shouts, taking his parade right up to my door. He is operating a new business and this change alone affords a triumphal return by actual train, one of the first trains to stop at our station, in fact, the very first being full of old politicians and young men of industry who only spoke from the caboose and did not get off. He is as proud of that train as he is of the *Fast Foot* he will soon be demonstrating, the first bicycle made in the United States, the safety bicycle, he says. He wrangles three of them to a stop at the front of my shop.

The perambulator of the future, he tells his crowd. He would have sold these bicycles at the last stop but people wanted to mount them and ride them away as soon as they were purchased, they didn't want to buy something they had to learn to ride. What does it take to ride a horse? he had asked them, he begged them to think of a horse. Learning to ride a bicycle takes no time at all in comparison.

Oh, the hoots and the yells!

The boy has slipped out of the shop to mill with the others. The peddler ropes the bicycles tight together as if they were wild horses and beckons the boy forward. Together they herd the bicycles around the side of the shop, bedeviled and blocked by the crowd and its questions: What if your foot catches in the turning? What is the trick to the wheels? How far can you pedal—my Uncle Zeke says one of them will go twenty miles, is that true? Do you fall on your head when you hit a rock?

The peddler answers nothing. He announces to the crowd that at three p.m. sharp they can return for the demonstration but no sooner. He tells the boy to secure the bicycles with this chain to a tree. Of course the crowd follows him into the orchard, pestering him. Boy, the peddler tells him, Beat them off.

Back, the boy shouts as if he has always shouted. The crowd is so surprised at such volume out of him they do step back, then a couple of his friends help him clear the crowd just so they can touch the handlebars.

No sooner than three in the afternoon, scowls the peddler. Then he eases himself up onto the boardwalk, enters my store this time and puts out the Closed sign.

He idles in front of my counter, calling out Miz Harriet

slow and pretty, as if he were drawing the name out of a bucket of honey. I let him call. I am not so excited to see him. After all that he said against me and my coming here, out of sheer jealousy? And I have had to restock from others all this time for more money, with new customers as well to do for. And surely he has heard about Henry.

That must be why he is so bold.

I fetch the baby from the bed and face him down.

A girl? he says.

She shows my own fair face, not Henry's mutton-chopped mug. I pull her to standing on the counter, and she wobbles forward, the way they do with their legs down solid, even so young. The peddler strokes her foot and tells me he considers her a duplicate, more stock. He will even sacrifice a twist of peppermint he says he has been saving since Cincinnati.

She is too new for your sweets, I tell him, folding her close. She is not yet even baptized, though the priest should be here in a week or so.

The peddler touches his curls at the mention of the priest. What about the boy? He will want the sweet.

You ask him, I say. You've got him there out back.

He cocks his head, looking at the twist still in his hand. Do you think the boy has it in him to learn to ride? I need a yahoo to show the others how easy it is. Such an opportunity is rare for a boy his age.

Opportunity is always waiting for a boy his age, I say.

The peddler toys with the peppermint. He doesn't look at me.

I hear these contraptions need a blacksmith to minister to them at every turning. They are held together with a lick and a promise, I say.

The peddler unwraps the candy and eats it. I am doing you a service, he says. These bicycles will be easy to sell once the boy learns how to ride and demonstrate its utility. And taking orders for this modern improvement in transportation will provide a good commission and no doubt increase your overall sales tenfold with customers coming inside to view it. You may need an increase of sales, he says, pointing at the baby.

You want to take the boy, I say.

There's a hard tap at the window. The crowd outside requires the peddler's attention, insists the bicycles be brought back, they are crazy about the bicycles, the boy doesn't know a thing about them.

There are many other boys, says the peddler.

An actual curtain of blossom hangs low all around my young orchard, blossoms that cast anybody under them elsewhere. The boy is whistling a little aria, not solely because his whistling drowns out any of the crowd not yet gone away, or any of the baby's cries he might have to attend to, but because he is wall-eyed by the size of the wheels he's guarding. His friends have deserted him in his triumph, they sense they will not play a part, they get bored, waiting, they will be back at three.

He can already feel the air rushing past his ears if and when he can get the wheels to turn under him. He hums a little while he feels the tires—real rubber!—and touches the rims as if they were burning his fingers in revolution.

With the door banging, the peddler arrives and unchains one of them. The boy mounts it with another whistle, but stops in distress when it can't be denied that his feet won't reach the pedals.

The peddler curses, turning in a circle. Then he calms down, claims that there is no problem, a boy grows so quickly, maybe he could try it again next year, maybe there is another boy with legs of the correct length in the town. The boy dismounts and stands with the peddler under the white blossoms looking at the bicycle propped just so, with the river and the train tracks beyond it. Wait, he says.

The peddler finds his pipe, lights a bowl. It will take him no time to find someone else. He can wait.

The boy runs back with leather strips and blocks of wood. He straps the wood to his feet with the leather.

You are such a wonder! shouts the peddler, taking a step back, scattering tobacco while the boy thumps across the ground on the shoe extensions. He mounts the contraption with them, settles clumsily to the pedals. He has to ride now, he has no choice. The peddler shoves him away from the tree.

Don't look at your feet, he shouts, look ahead and use the handles, grip them like a bull's horns, and pedal—that's it.

He falls.

The peddler commends the boy, he tells the boy how hard it is not to fall because the orchard bulges everywhere with tree roots. But even deeper ruts run in the main street due to the recent rain, he reminds him. Once you conquer it though, he says—he looks at his watch—it is simple, ruts and whatever else, you will ride over it all. Ten minutes of two, he says. You will learn this in no time, says the peddler, clapping him on the shoulder. A good boy like you.

Some never learn, such as himself.

Sometimes the boy is still working at the pedals when he falls. His nose starts to bleed the third time he goes down and his shin is soon torn but he seems to be getting it. The peddler hopes he is getting it. The peddler is out of breath and his back aches from holding the seat steady, running along with the bicycle at the beginning of each try.

At last, for no reason other than it is a miracle of wooden blocks and balance, the boy rides a distance upright. The peddler wipes the boy's nose with a kerchief drenched with the sweat of his worry, and proceeds to wheel him out of the orchard down onto the street. It is ten after three.

Even the women trading eggs and loiterers who drag a broom across the boardwalk now and then have gathered, along with a good portion of the town. The peddler aims the boy into one of the deepest ruts that line the street—and he rides. Some people on the street clap their hands to their mouths, they can't believe it, then they clap for him. Even the rougher boys give him room. It is a miracle all the boys want the secret to.

It takes only a few minutes of your time to learn—and then you are repaid by a lifetime of travel! the peddler shouts, running after him. Before they can see how the boy is beginning to wobble, he cups his hands around his mouth to be sure I can hear him from where I stand beside my window and shouts, Orders at Miz Harriet's.

Chapter 29

I prick myself sewing the peddler's lace onto the baby's baptismal dress but I don't notice the blood for several more stitches, the sun is so low and red, I don't notice it in this light until there's a red streak under a whole row, I don't notice it because there's a speck of red like an eye's irritation in the corner of my eye floating out the window. The balloon has returned, and its red ball has been lofting and floating, swelling in the sky all day. Even anchored some ways off, I can see it. Its route follows the train's—but skips us.

It hasn't stopped here again in all this time.

The boy runs in while I am filling a basin with cold water to soak the red out of the dress.

It's the last night, he says. He's short of breath from showing a farmer and his sons how well this bicycle of his follows a furrow.

I push the cloth into the water and rub at the stain. I told you—we have a baby now and cannot run off to every amusement.

That baby, says the boy, and he balls his fists.

Just forget that the balloon is there. You wouldn't even

know there was an opera attached to it except for the flyers they drop.

But I do know. The neighbors said they would give me a ride to hear it. I can ride with them, he says. They already said they were going. They have room for me on the buckboard.

No.

I haven't heard the opera but once, that first time.

And this is the last I want to hear about it.

But why? The boy stretches out *Why* until it's as long as his thirteen-year-old self.

I want to hit him and hold him. I have my reasons, I say.

He says nothing to match my nothing.

You can attend the next one that comes here twice, I say, scrubbing the lace in the pink-tinted water.

But I want to go now, he says. He is too old to stomp his boots, but kept-back sobs slur his words in rising anger. The peddler wants me to go too, to show the bicycle.

I wring the lace dry. No, I say.

You are not even my mother, he shouts, and he runs out door, banging it so it hits the latch hard.

I grab the baby by her nightshirt and tuck her under one arm. By the time I get the door open he's not anywhere in front. I limp around the side and catch sight of the last of him—he's too quick now, a quarter mile away, flying along the ruts beside the river, peddling as hard as he can.

Coveys of quail skitter up in the new evening-pale light.

Hush, baby, I say. He's old enough.

I don't cry at the loss of the boy, the boy of my true life, the boy heavy on my back when I needed him, the boy who kept me here instead of wandering after Pa. In the morning I dress the baby in all her baptismal lace, I carry her down to the river a good hour before the priest is due.

I tell her I always thought I would have Pa in a child if I had one—but here she is, a girl like myself. Take this water, my little Duschecka, don't cry now—this is the *I baptize you* the way I do it.

In the name of your father who is gone, I say out loud, the son who is not mine, and the holy ghost who is Pa. Out with the devil, I say, and I flinch. I look into the sky where I last saw that balloon an hour ago but the sky now extends open and empty, as clear as a witness to a soul-claiming should be.

Now you have heard your real name, little Duschecka, and not the one I will tell the priest to give you. I will have your photograph taken standing on my lap for the boy to put in a locket. I don't need to look into the flat of the river to see that the photographer will have to lighten my face to make it something a boy could show. But when I part my hair by the shine of a pan, I part it straight, Duschecka, and so will you.

In the Flyover Fiction series

Ordinary Genius
Thomas Fox Averill

Jackalope Dreams
Mary Clearman Blew

Reconsidering Happiness: A Novel
Sherrie Flick

The Usual Mistakes
Erin Flanagan

The Floor of the Sky
Pamela Carter Joern

The Plain Sense of Things
Pamela Carter Joern

Stolen Horses
Dan O'Brien

Because a Fire Was in My Head
Lynn Stegner

Bohemian Girl
Terese Svoboda

Tin God
Terese Svoboda

Another Burning Kingdom
Robert Vivian

Lamb Bright Saviors
Robert Vivian

The Mover of Bones
Robert Vivian

The Sacred White Turkey
Frances Washburn

Skin
Kellie Wells

To order or obtain more information on these or other University of Nebraska Press titles, visit www.nebraskapress.unl.edu.

Other Works by Terese Svoboda

POETRY

All Aberration

Laughing Africa

Mere Mortals

Treason

Weapons Grade

FICTION

Cannibal

A Drink Called Paradise

Trailer Girl and Other Stories

Tin God

Pirate Talk or Mermalade

MEMOIR

Black Glasses like Clark Kent

TRANSLATION

Cleaned the Crocodile's Teeth: Nuer Song